What the Hex

THE GRAVESTONE MYSTERIES — BOOK THREE

JANE HINCHEY

BAYWOLF PRESS

BP

BAYWOLF PRESS

What the Hex © 2023 Jane Hinchey

Editor: Paula Lester

Cover Designer: Lou Harper, Cover Affairs

This is a work of fiction. Names, characters, businesses, places, events and incidents are either the products of the author's imagination or used in a fictitious manner. Any resemblance to actual persons, living or dead, or actual events is purely coincidental.

WHAT THE HEX

**Secrets and soul stones and neon body paint...
guess who's up to her neck in murder?**

Just when undercover SIA agent Holly Day thinks
she has life in small town Gravestone handled,
someone flies off the handle and Tarkath mobster
Dino Cittadino turns up dead.

Throw in a treasure hunt with fake clues, a busty
blonde with secrets of her own, and a mysterious
stranger who seems oddly familiar, and Holly is up
to her eyeballs in intrigue and chaos.

Holly's mission? Avoid trouble and keep a low
profile.

Holly's reality? She's on a rollercoaster ride of danger, where she can't go five minutes without getting injured, and the only thing hotter than the murder investigation is her crush on the sheriff.

Life has become messier than a kid's finger-painting project, more complicated than advanced calculus, and more dangerous than running with scissors. And that's just a typical day for Holly! Her rat, Flynn, is her only constant companion in this whirlwind of madness, and her senior sidekick Doris is always ready to risk life and limb - or at least her driver's license - to help Holly solve the case. Holly's life is a swirling vortex of chaos. All she can do is hold on for dear life and hope she doesn't get splattered like a bug on a windshield.

CHAPTER ONE

Thunder rumbled overhead, dark and ominous, matching my mood perfectly.

"You think we'll make it, Flynn?" I asked the rat currently riding shotgun in the basket on my handlebars. "Or are we about to get wet?"

Flynn squeaked, the breeze from our mad pedal along the foreshore ruffling his fur.

"I agree," I puffed, pedaling harder, my thighs burning as I attempted to outrun the storm. It had been folly to go out at all, but I'd had to leave the house or go crazy, for every little creak and groan of the decrepit old cottage had me on edge. I was jumping at shadows. A bike ride had seemed a good idea, despite the ever-darkening skies. Anything to burn off the restless sense of dread dogging my heels.

The only breeze was that of our own making, the air heavy, oppressive, and still. Sweat soaked my tank and shorts in unflattering patches, but thankfully no one was around to see. One fat raindrop landed on the back of my hand. Then another.

"Brace yourself, Flynn. It's about to get moist."

Understatement of the year. The heavens opened in a torrential downpour, soaking us within seconds. On the up-side, there was no need to worry about those unflattering sweat stains anymore. Flynn squeaked and curled himself into a ball in the bottom of the basket, as if making himself as small as possible would prevent the rain from reaching him. It didn't.

Keeping one hand firmly on the handlebars, I used the other to wipe the rain from my eyes, blinded by the deluge as it fell heavy and hard. I didn't see the pothole, but I sure felt it when my front wheel bounced into the crater and stayed there, bringing the bike to an abrupt halt and wrenching the handlebars out of my grip.

"Hold on!" I screamed to Flynn as I parted company with the bicycle, tumbling onto the road with the groan of bending metal and the sting of flesh on asphalt. Dazed, I scrambled to my feet, limping to the bike that lay with the front wheel buckled. "Great," I grumbled, not relishing the walk home. The whole reason I'd taken the bike was because I was still wearing my walking boot, my broken navicular not fully healed.

"Flynn?" I bent toward the basket, hoping Flynn had heard my yell and held on and hadn't been catapulted onto the road.

The sodden, bedraggled ball of fur was fine. Outraged but fine. Upon seeing me, he unfurled and stood on his back legs, front legs waving as he squeaked up a storm. I figured he was using every cuss word known to man by the way his tirade went on and on and his tail flicked in displeasure. I bit my lips and tried not to smile at the sight he made, one angry, wet, unhappy rat, cussing me out.

"Finished?" I asked when he eventually wound down. He nodded. "Are you hurt?" He shook his head, then pointed to my knee, which was stinging like the devil. A quick glance told me what I already knew. Blood mixed with water ran down my shin from a nasty graze.

"Yeah, I know." I sighed, then showed him my elbow. "Got one here too."

He made a clicking noise, as if tsking me for my foolishness.

"Yeah, yeah, I know that too. Come on, let's get home before my luck really does run out and I get struck by lightning." Reaching down, I scooped Flynn up and positioned him on my shoulder, where he held onto my hair for balance while I picked up the bike. Doris wasn't going to be happy that I'd wrecked it. She'd lent it to me so I could get around until my walking boot came off.

Despite the bent and buckled front wheel, the bike made a handy crutch as we limped along the shore, heads bent against the rain. I'd yet to see another soul and had resigned myself to the fact that we were going to have to walk the entire way instead of hitching a lift when I saw something that made me pause.

"*Squeak?*" Flynn tugged on my hair, wanting to know why we'd stopped.

"Someone's in the rotunda." I pointed. There was a figure all right, only whoever it was? They were lying on the ground. "Quick, they may be hurt." I hurried as fast as my broken foot, bent wheel, and the rain would allow.

Who could it be? Someone as crazy as I was to be out in this storm, that was for sure. Maybe they'd been caught in the rain too, and had sought shelter in the rotunda, only they'd slipped, and now lay helpless. Which made me think of Doris. Let's face it, despite her past life as an SIA agent—now retired— she was a woman in her seventies. It wouldn't take much to break a hip.

Letting the bike fall to the ground, I used the handrail to haul myself up the steps. Shaking off excess water and wiping moisture from my eyes, I regarded the figure on the ground, goosebumps prickling my skin. It wasn't Doris. It was Dino Cittadino, and he was very much dead.

Flynn squeaked again and shot down my arm before leaping to the ground and onto Dino's leg.

"Flynn," I warned, but he couldn't hear me because the rain thundered on the tin roof so loudly my ears hurt. Cautiously, I approached, skirting around the body, examining it from every angle. It wasn't that I was concerned Dino wasn't really dead and was about to come at me at any second. I was one hundred percent confident Dino's heart had been removed, judging by the way his chest had been ripped open. And *that* was downright concerning.

Wrenching my eyes from the sight, I looked out, first over the ocean and then toward the row of shops directly opposite, not yet open. Squinting through the sheets of rain, I considered my options. I could just leave. Pretend I'd never stumbled upon him. Tempting, but I wasn't sure I could do it. Which meant I had to alert the authorities and embroil myself in yet another Gravestone mystery. Harding had warned me to lie low. *This* was not lying low.

Kneeling by Dino's side, I began patting down his pockets, ignoring the throbbing in my grazed knee and elbow and the fact that I was no doubt leaving blood at the crime scene. Flynn squeaked, head cocked to one side.

"I'm looking for clues," I shouted, to be heard over the rain. "Because I'm going to have to call this in, and no doubt, Deputy Biden will arrest me for killing him." It wouldn't be the first time the overzealous deputy had wrongly thrown me in a cell, and it probably wouldn't be the last. She was an arrest first, ask questions later kinda law-woman. "We may as well save some time and go about finding his killer ourselves." Because I was curious. Who'd managed to take down this Tarkath mobster? And more curiously, why? Although that was probably a stupid question. The Tarkaths had enemies. Dino's death could easily be retribution for some transgression either he or another Tarkath were responsible for.

Flynn considered what I'd said, nodded, and began sniffing at Dino's clothing. While rifling through his pockets, I examined his face. His skin was gray, lips blue, and placing the back of my fingers against his cheek, I confirmed what I suspected. His body was cold. "He's been dead for hours. Possibly since last night." Because why else would Dino Cittadino be in the rotunda other than some clandestine meeting in the dead of night? Heck, Dino didn't even live here. Last I'd heard, he'd left Gravestone in his rearview. To find him here, like this, was a shock. Especially given our history.

Turning my attention back to his trouser pocket, I pulled out his phone. The screen was dark, but a swipe of my finger had it lighting up.

"It's locked. Shouldn't be a problem though. It uses facial recognition." I held it up to Dino's face. Nothing. I changed the angle, first one way, then another. "What do you think, Flynn? Either it doesn't recognize a dead face or, more probable, his eyes need to be open."

Flynn stiffened, then shook his head, his ears flattening.

I looked from the phone to Dino. Swallowing, I reached out and, using my forefinger and thumb, pried an eyelid open. My mouth filled with saliva, and I thought I was going to gag. "This is so gross," I whispered, holding the phone up to Dino's face once more. It didn't unlock.

"You've got to be kidding me!" With my stomach heaving, I reached over and pried open his other eye. "There. Both eyes open. Happy now?" I was, of course, speaking to the phone, which I held up for a third and final time. It did not unlock.

"Gah!" I wailed, nausea burning my throat. Swiping my palm over his eyes to close them, I sat back, gulping in great breaths of air until the impending urge to vomit passed.

Sliding the phone into the back pocket of my shorts, I continued the search. Keys. The remnants of a pack of gum. Nothing remotely interesting, not even a weapon.

"Got anything?" I asked Flynn.

"Squeak."

Not knowing if that was a yes or a no, I groaned and hauled myself to my feet, hobbling to Flynn, who was attempting to uncurl Dino's fingers, which were clenched around a scrap of paper.

"This looks promising." Lowering myself to the floor, I took over. The scrap of paper was a flyer for a treasure hunt happening in Gravestone this coming weekend. But it wasn't the flyer that held my attention. It was what was carved into Dino's palm.

"Do you see?" I whispered, and despite the deluge of rain and rumbling of thunder, Flynn heard, for he squeaked a response.

"It's the same rune." Flattening Dino's palm, I pulled out my phone and snapped photos of the rune carved into his hand. It was fresh, the cuts shallow. It was the same rune Denise Hurt used to place a death hex on Seth Saltzman and John Smith. Only Denise had been caught and locked away, so who had carved up Dino?

"Someone is practicing dark magic," I murmured, taking photos of Dino's chest and the gaping wound. I bent my head closer, ignoring the coppery scent of blood because there was something else, another odor underneath that shouldn't have been there. "What is that? Can you smell it?" I asked Flynn. He climbed onto Dino's collarbone, nose and whiskers twitching.

"Is it…" I breathed in, closing my eyes, zeroing in on the scent. "Belladonna?" I whispered, eyes popping open. Flynn nodded in agreement. "Not only deadly, but it can regulate the heart rate," I surprised myself by saying. I didn't recall how I knew that, but I was kinda grateful I knew it at all.

"Look here." I pointed to the edges of the wound. "I mean, I'm not sticking my hand in there to find out for sure, but I'd bet you anything his heart is missing. But this wound? Not surgical. Not done with a sharp instrument. The edges of his skin almost look as if they were torn. And look—" I pointed to a faint trace of red powder dusting the area around the wound. "Any ideas on what this substance is?"

I raised my eyes to Flynn, who shrugged. Chewing my lip, I thought for a moment. I had two choices. Call this in now and let Calder and Biden work the case. Or take what I'd discovered and investigate myself. I mean, really; it wasn't a hard decision.

Holding out my hand, palm out, I instructed Flynn. "Pass me that flyer."

Flynn leaped off Dino, grabbed the flyer, and placed it in my hand. Carefully, I scraped up as much of the red powder as I could, then folded the paper, securing the powder inside. It joined Dino's phone in my back pocket. What Gravestone PD didn't know wouldn't hurt them.

I took more photos than I needed, both of Dino's body and the rotunda, then one final pat down of the body, which was when I discovered the dagger strapped to his ankle.

He *did* have a weapon. But the blade was holstered, indicating Dino either hadn't been fast enough to retrieve it, or he hadn't suspected whoever he was meeting was a threat. Deciding to leave the dagger where it was, I tugged Dino's trouser leg back into place, then backed away.

Lifting my phone, I dialed.

CHAPTER TWO

Deputy Laura Biden charged across the grass toward the rotunda, wet weather gear glistening. The lights on her patrol car flashed blue and red, distorted by the rain.

I'd dragged my bike up against the steps, sheltering it as much as possible from the weather, with Flynn hiding in the basket. The deputy paid it no mind, mounting the steps two at a time, her face a study of fierce determination. Shaking the rain from her jacket, her eyes swept over Dino, her mouth dropping open before she could hide her reaction. Snapping it closed, she stepped toward me, crowding in close, intimidation radiating from her in waves.

"What happened here?" she growled.

"Well, at first glance," I drawled, "I'd say someone murdered Dino Cittadino, deputy." Probably wasn't the smartest move to sass her. She puffed up like a bantam rooster and was ready to read me the riot act when the whoop of a siren had her changing her mind and stepping back. Over her shoulder, I watched as Calder pulled his truck in behind the deputy's patrol car.

"Cavalry's here," I muttered under my breath. Luckily, the rain belting on the tin roof drowned out my words, saving me from another berating from the woman who took her job way too seriously. Feigning a casualness I didn't feel, I watched Calder climb from his truck and pull his hat down low to fend off the torrential rain. His long, denim-clad legs ate up the distance in no time, and I reluctantly dragged my gaze from his lithe form to the street where they'd parked.

"Will it flood, do you think?" My concern was real. The rain was heavy and unrelenting, although admittedly, Gravestone had the uncanny ability to attract more storms and inclement weather than any other town in Texas and had survived each one with minimal disruption.

Calder shook his hat and ran his hands through his hair before positioning the baseball cap with the Gravestone PD emblem back on his head. "Not yet."

"Has it flooded before?"

"Back in..." He paused, looked up at the roof of the rotunda as if the answer was there. "Oh, must've been ninety-four? Mild flooding. Relax, we've got nothing to worry about. This is just a summer shower."

Deputy Biden cleared her throat, no doubt annoyed we were chit chatting about the weather when there was a dead body at our feet. I wanted to say she could relax; he wasn't going to get any deader, but I bit my tongue. As tempting as it was to rile her, I didn't fancy spending time in a cell today. Truth was, besides being dripping wet, my grazed knee and elbow hurt like the devil, and I badly —*badly*—needed a coffee. Let's not mention Dino's phone and the mysterious substance I'd swiped a sample of were practically burning a hole in my back pocket.

"What do we have, deputy?" Calder turned his full attention to the crime scene.

"Blood here. Fresh. Possibly cast off from the injury." She pointed to where I'd kneeled by Dino's side. I didn't mean to roll my eyes, but honestly? Anyone could see the blood she was pointing at hadn't come from Dino—the blood around his wound had congealed and partially dried, whereas the blood on the floor was fresh. Not to mention the damp patches where the rain had dripped off me.

Calder glanced at the bloodstain, then me, his eyes zeroing in on my knee. "You're hurt."

I shrugged. "Came off my bike." I jerked my thumb toward the bicycle with the warped front wheel. "Took a bit of skin off." I held up my elbow to show him the matching graze.

He stepped closer, close enough that my heart stuttered for a second before resuming in double time. When his fingers curled around my upper arm, I could have sworn it stopped altogether. Anyone would think I had cardiac issues the way my heart behaved around this man. With electricity sparking where he touched, I prayed I wouldn't embarrass myself and swoon.

"That looks painful."

"Yup."

"You touched the body?" Deputy Biden sounded scandalized.

"I checked his pulse." The lie rolled off my tongue as smooth as silk. Calder sighed, and I raised my eyes to his. Of course, he knew I was lying. I liked to think it was a thing between us now, that I'd lie and he'd acknowledge it in a good-natured manner, and we'd move on.

"Tell me what happened," Calder said. "Why are you out in such weather?"

"It wasn't raining when I left home," I protested, although he had a valid point. Any fool could see a storm was rolling in, but I wasn't about to admit I was a fool. "It's simple really." I smiled sweetly. At least I hoped it was sweetly. Before coming to Gravestone, I'd barely smiled at all, so my facial muscles were in shock at these new expressions I was inflicting on them. Admittedly, some of my smiles were more like snarls and baring of teeth. "I was out for a ride when it started to rain. Then I hit a pothole." I jerked my thumb toward the twisted front wheel of my bicycle. "Figured I'd seek shelter under the rotunda until the rain stopped, and that's when I found it was already occupied."

Calder studied me for a long, silent moment, his hazel eyes with their flecks of gold mesmerizing. They really were quite pretty. I'd never thought of anyone's eyes as pretty before, let alone a man's eyes, but Sheriff Joshua Calder definitely had pretty eyes. Maybe even sexy eyes. Dare I say, bedroom eyes?

I realized he'd spoken and was waiting for an answer.

"Sorry, what?" I cupped a hand behind my ear. "Didn't hear you over the rain."

He smirked, not buying it. "I said, do you think Doris could give you a lift home? I'd get the deputy to take you, but she's needed here."

"Pretty sure Doris would be delighted. So, I'm free to go?" It was almost anticlimactic.

He nodded, then added, "Don't leave town."

I let out a snort, already hitting speed dial on my phone.

"Mornin' Holly," Doris answered on the second ring. "What's up?"

"I need a lift." I'd decided bad news was best delivered fast, so I continued with barely a breath, "I crashed your bike and busted up the front wheel, and now I'm stuck at the rotunda."

Doris, to my relief, laughed. "Wouldn't be the first time she's been dinged up, won't be the last. Hang ten, I'll be right there."

I hung up to discover the deputy shooting me daggers.

"What?" I protested. Geez, you couldn't catch a break with this woman.

"You're contaminating the crime scene," she scolded. "You're going to have to wait outside."

"Outside?" I jerked my thumb toward the torrential downpour behind me. "In the rain?"

"You're already wet," she pointed out. You know, I was just about to do what she asked because honestly, I wasn't in the mood for the deputy today, and she had a valid point. I *was* already wet. But Calder intervened.

"That won't be necessary, Laura. You're fine to wait here until Doris arrives."

I shot him a *don't do me any favors* look but was secretly grateful I wasn't being forced to stand outside. I was uncomfortable as it was. Thankfully, Doris drove like she was in the Daytona and pulled up a few short minutes later.

"My ride's here." I waved goodbye and hobbled down the stairs, head bent against the rain. If Calder or the deputy replied, I didn't hear them, intent on getting out of there before either of them noticed the bulge in my back pocket and realized I'd swiped Dino's phone.

Doris waved as I approached and popped the trunk. "Throw her in the back!" she yelled. Flynn resumed his usual position on my shoulder while I finagled the bicycle into the trunk—thank goodness Doris had an Impala or it would never have fit.

Soaked to the skin, I opened the passenger door and gingerly lowered myself onto the seat. "Sorry, I'm wet."

"Here." A towel hit me in the face. "I came prepared. So, what's going on? Why the cops?"

After patting my face dry and squeezing what moisture I could from my hair, I looked at her, then did a double take. "Why are you covered in neon body paint?"

"Best not to ask."

I snorted. "Right."

Throwing the Impala into gear, she swung the wheel, narrowly missing Calder's truck as she pulled onto the road.

"Spill. What's up with that?" She jerked her thumb toward the crime scene behind us.

"I just found Dino Cittadino's body. He was murdered."

"And you're not in jail? Progress."

"I know, right?" I threw her a grin. I liked Doris. She was the first real friend I'd had in… forever. Despite the holes in my memory, I sensed I'd never had a close friendship with another person in a very long time, if at all, and I assumed it was because of my job as an SIA agent. Of course, there were probably other reasons too. I just couldn't remember what they were.

"I didn't know Dino was back in town," Doris said, leaning forward and squinting. The windshield wipers flapped back and forth, doing little to displace the heavy rain. She eased her foot off the accelerator a fraction, and I gave a silent prayer of thanks.

"Me either. I figured he met someone at the rotunda last night, and whoever it was killed him. But"—I paused and drew in a long breath—"I have concerns."

"You have concerns? What, that Dino is dead? I didn't think you liked him?"

"I don't, and no, not that. Doris? This was a ritualistic killing."

"As in?"

"Blood magic. Or at least dark magic."

She slammed on the brakes so hard I catapulted forward, my seatbelt catching me before I connected with the windshield. Flynn, using my hair as a rope, swung out in front of me from one shoulder to the other as if he were Tarzan in the frigging jungle. "Jeez," I wheezed, rubbing at the welt across my collarbone. "Take it easy, would ya?"

"Sorry." She moved her foot from the brake back to the accelerator, and we resumed our journey. "Tell me everything. What makes you think it was blood magic?"

I told her about the symbol carved into Dino's palm, the mysterious red powder, the smell of Belladonna, and my very strong suspicion that his heart was missing. I also fessed up to stealing his phone, to which she leaned over and slapped my thigh, hard, and grinned. "Atta girl!"

Moving my weight to my left butt cheek, I tugged the phone and scrunched up flyer out of my shorts pocket, both slightly damp.

"What's that?" Doris zeroed in on the flyer, nearly running us off the road before jerking the wheel and getting us back on course.

"Flynn found this flyer for the treasure hunt clenched in Dino's hand. I used it to scoop up some of the powder, figured we could try to work out what it was, where it came from, you know—"

"—usual SIA stuff," Doris finished, eyes sparkling.

"Stuff that I'm sure the sheriff wouldn't appreciate us sticking our noses in," I agreed, unable to stop the smile. Doris missed the turn off to my street, instead executing a seven-point turn and heading in the opposite direction. Before I could ask, she said, "You can dry off at my place. We've got time to clean up before the meeting—and maybe enough time to crack that phone and identify the powder, all before morning tea."

"That's this morning?" I was losing track of time. I could have sworn the meeting was tomorrow.

CHAPTER THREE

"Quick, look busy!" Doris hissed, hurriedly tossing napkins onto the table.

"I am busy," I shot back, wondering for the millionth time how I'd gotten roped into helping with the latest Gravestone Women's Committee meeting. The meetings used to be a social gathering of, you guessed it, the womenfolk of Gravestone, where they'd sit around drinking tea and solving the town's problems in the form of gossip. Until Kerris Jones, the mayor, had elbowed her way in, taken over the committee, and now used the group to do her bidding.

"I thought you weren't coming to these meetings anymore," I said, placing a tray of cookies on the table. I'd taken a quick shower at Doris's house and had sat wrapped in a towel, trying to unlock Dino's phone, while my clothes were in the dryer. Doris had also showered and removed the neon body paint, refusing to be drawn on what she'd been doing to end up covered in it. I figured that one was best left alone and instead I'd given her the task of identifying the powder.

I hadn't been able to unlock the phone, and Doris hadn't been able to identify the red powder. Our investigating so far had brought up bupkis.

"It's not every day the chairwoman calls a special meeting and issues an open invitation," Doris said. "I'm curious as to why."

"You don't think she got wind of the Keen Agers, do you?" The Keen Agers was the new group Doris had formed, consisting of women over seventy, with no affiliation to the Gravestone Council. So far, they'd kept the group a secret from Kerris. I figured once she got wind of it, she'd probably pass some sort of bylaw forbidding the formation of social groups or some such thing.

Doris shrugged, scooping a handful of snacks into her purse. "I doubt it."

"I saw that, Doris," Sheriff Joshua Calder said from behind me, making me jump. "Appropriating group snacks for personal use."

"I like to call it *appropriating* the snacks into my purse," Doris said.

"Or, as I like to call it, theft," he shot back.

I spun to face him. "What are you doing here?" This was the Gravestone Women's Committee. Emphasis on the women. Which he most definitely was not. Plus, he had a murder to investigate. Why was he here when he had much more important duties to attend to?

Let's not mention how, whenever he walked into a room, my heart did somersaults and my breath hitched in my throat. You could be forgiven for thinking I was having some sort of medical episode whenever he was near. I was part appalled and part intrigued by the phenomena that was my reaction to this man.

"Nice to see you too, Holly," he teased, dimple flashing. Heat scorched my cheeks, and I busied myself rearranging cookies on the tray. "Actually, Kerris invited me to talk with you all," Calder said.

"About?"

Before he could answer, the doors burst open, and a crowd of women rushed into the room, Kerris in the lead. Calder touched my hand in farewell and went to join her, while my eyes tracked his every move.

"You're drooling." Doris nudged me in the ribs, and I raised a hand to my mouth in horror. Thankfully, there was no drool, but honestly, I wouldn't have been surprised if there had been. Calder was hot with a capital H, and I wasn't immune.

"Do you think he's here to interrogate us about Dino's murder?" I asked the elderly woman by my side who was still pilfering snacks.

"Doubtful." She shrugged. "This meeting was planned before Dino's demise. Have to admit, I'm surprised to see him here."

"Thank you, ladies." Kerris raised her voice to be heard over the chatter. "Please, take your seats." She assumed her position at the head of the huge board room table—the meetings now took place in the formal setting of the council chambers rather than members' kitchen tables. Calder remained standing off to one side. Our eyes met, and I was hard pressed to look away.

Kerris was saying something about declaring the meeting open and blathering on about recent events. It wasn't until she gave Calder the floor that I paid attention.

"Ladies, I'll keep this brief." He smiled, his eyes twinkling and his dimple flashing, and I heard every woman around the table sigh, utterly smitten with the sheriff. "There's a treasure hunt coming to Gravestone, and with events like these, well, as exciting as they are, they can also attract an unwanted and unwelcome element. The mayor and I think it's pertinent to remind you about stranger danger, to be aware of your surroundings, and to be mindful that not everyone can be trusted."

Silence settled over the women as we digested his words. I wasn't concerned with stranger danger. I *was* concerned with the mention of the treasure hunt, since I'd found the flyer advertising the event clasped in dead Dino's hand. How was it connected? Was Dino here for the community event? He didn't seem the community spirited kind. No, I was pretty sure Dino was intending to use the treasure hunt as a cover. The big question was, for what? Another concern niggled. I was lying low, in hiding, and Gravestone was perfect for it, but the more outsiders who visited, the higher my risk of discovery.

"What's the treasure?" Carrie DeSofa asked.

Before Calder could answer, Kerris jumped in, her tone condescending. "It's not real treasure, Carrie. It's a series of puzzles and challenges that contestants take part in."

"Some people are such treasures you just want to

bury them," Doris whispered, and I almost laughed out loud, smothering my smile behind my hand.

Ada Rose Bartlett raised her hand, and Calder nodded at her. "Yes, Ada?"

"Are you going to teach us self-defense?" Her tone was hopeful, and I swung my gaze back to Calder, wondering if that was what he was really here for.

I wasn't entirely surprised when he said, "Yes." Then he looked directly at me. "Holly? Care to join me? I need a volunteer."

Caught between a rock and a hard place, he left me with little option other than to agree. Pushing back my chair, I stood. "Sure." I limped toward him, my walking boot muffled by the carpeted floor. My skinned knee and elbow were appropriately bandaged, thanks to Doris's first aid kit.

"I'm really not sure Holly should do this." Ethel chewed a nail, a worried expression on her face. "She's already injured, and well, no disrespect, Calder, but you're a big guy and she's a girl…"

Once I reached his side, Calder indicated my broken foot. "This is exactly why I chose Holly. You all agree she's an easy target, yes? She can't run away, or at least not very fast, because she has an injury."

Nods of agreement from everyone present.

"You've all seen a wildlife documentary where the predators seek the weakest prey?"

More murmuring and head nodding. They could see where he was going with this. He wanted to prove to them that even the weakest link had a chance of survival if armed with the right tools. Or weapons. Of which I was devoid. The problem was, he wanted me to play the victim, a role that didn't sit well with me. I had to remind myself—for the millionth time—that I was here undercover and if I didn't want the sweet women in front of me to discover the truth, then I'd better brush up on my acting skills.

"Hands up! Who's seen *Miss Congeniality?*" Calder asked, and almost every hand shot up in the air. "Remember S.I.N.G? Solar plexus, instep, nose, groin."

He stood to my side and performed the actions. "Solar plexus—you ram your elbow into your assailant's stomach." He then stamped his foot. "Stomp on their foot, as hard as you can." Then he lifted his arm, fingers curled into a fist, and shot it backward. "Punch 'em in the nose. And then, your favorite, go for the groin."

Everyone giggled.

"Let's run through this for real. Ready, Holly? I'm

going to come from behind and grab you. Your goal is to get away, call for help."

I felt his heat as he moved in close behind me, the breath against my ear as he whispered, "Ready?" I gave a nod, then his arms wrapped around me, and all thoughts of S.I.N.G. flew out of my head and instinct took over. I elbowed him in the stomach, hard, and as his breath whooshed out, I reached up, grabbed him around the neck and, using my body as leverage, catapulted him over my shoulder. He flew through the air, landing on his back in front of me with a wheeze. There were shocked gasps and chairs pushing back as everyone rushed to see if Calder was okay.

I cast a panicked glance at Doris, not sure how I should handle things. It had been pure instinct and despite telling myself to play along with Calder's charade, I hadn't, and now everyone was looking at me, some with admiration, others with outright suspicion.

"Oops," Doris mouthed, and shrugged, palms up.

Holding out a hand to Calder, I helped him to his feet. "Sorry about that. You okay?"

"Oh, I'm fine, don't you worry about that. The question is, Miss Day, where did you learn a move like that?"

"I took a class once." Technically, not a lie.

Vera rolled up her sleeves. "I can take him. I took a self-defense class when I was fifteen." Vera was pushing eighty. The class she took when she was fifteen was a long time ago.

Calder placed a restraining hand on Vera's shoulder, keeping her in her seat. "That won't be necessary, Vera, but thank you. Remember, ladies, the goal isn't to win. It's to get away, to incapacitate your attacker long enough to run."

"I run like the winded," Gladys Overwith confessed, and laughter filled the room, breaking the tension.

"Ladies, before I go." Calder waved everyone to be quiet. "One last thing. Did anyone see Dino Cittadino in the last twenty-four hours?"

My gaze shot straight to Kerris, who was watching the sheriff with a curious expression on her face. "May I ask why you're asking, sheriff?" she inquired.

"Because he was found dead this morning. Murdered."

Gasps of shock and horror followed his words, then a series of denials that the women in the room hadn't known Dino was even in town, let alone seen or spoken to him. Kerris's hand shot to her throat, twisting the strand of pearls around her neck. Her face paled beneath the heavy mask of makeup she wore. Then a shutter came down over her face. Between one blink and the next, any emotion she displayed at the news of Dino's death was wiped away.

There was a knock at the door, and Kerris's assistant poked her head in. "I'm sorry to interrupt, Sheriff, but I have a resident on the phone who thinks her lawn is on fire."

To give Calder his due, he didn't bat an eyelid. "I'll be right there. Thank you, ladies. Stay safe, and if you think of anything that could assist in Dino's investigation, something you might have seen or heard, no matter how small or insignificant, please report it."

After he'd left and I'd returned to my seat, Kerris banged her gavel on the table to get our attention. "A bit of quiet, if you don't mind," she demanded over the chatter that had broken out. The woman made me curious. If you'd just found out the man you shared your bed with had been murdered, how would you act? Continue on with business as usual? Or let your emotions show? "You're not at home now. You're at council and decorum is insisted upon."

I could practically hear spines snapping as they immediately straightened, lips clamped shut and hands folded demurely. I glanced at Doris out of the corner of my eye, and she poked her tongue out. I sucked in my lips to keep from laughing.

Kerris kept us at the meeting for another hour. She briefly talked about the treasure hunt, telling us it was organized by an external party and therefore, there was no need for us to do anything. She then moved on to other business that I couldn't care less about until eventually we were free to leave.

"Finally," Doris grumbled, slinging her oversized purse over her shoulder and almost taking me out in the process. "What a colossal waste of time that was. The only good part was the five seconds of airtime Calder gave Dino's murder."

"You don't think learning self-defense is worthwhile? Not for us, of course, but for the others?" I jerked my head at the gray hair brigade filing out of the room ahead of us.

"I do. But this wasn't a class. It was a demonstration, sure, but these gals need hands on practice, not watching you toss Calder around like a rag doll. Not that it wasn't entertaining, but the whole thing screams of a setup and I wanna know why."

"What do you mean, a setup?" I hurried as fast as I could with my broken foot to keep pace with her.

Out on the sidewalk, she turned to me, gripping my shoulders. "Think about it. If the sheriff and the mayor thought this proposed treasure hunt was so dangerous, they wouldn't let it go ahead. The whole thing was a ruse."

She had a point. The announcement of the treasure hunt and segue into a self-defense demonstration had been… odd.

"A ruse for what?" I asked. "It couldn't have been for Dino's murder because the meeting had been arranged long before he'd been killed."

"Exactly!"

CHAPTER FOUR

"You should hold a class," Doris said, entering River's café ahead of me, the bell above the door announcing our arrival.

"What?" I frowned, having no idea what she was talking about.

"The whole self-defense thing." She waved a hand around randomly. "You should hold a class. You were too busy panicking to notice the women around the table. They all wanted to be you. They all want to learn those badass moves."

"Knowing how to punch someone in the face isn't going to save you from a hex," I pointed out. "Or black magic."

She cocked her head. "You've got a point."

My eyes landed on a leggy blonde across the

room. "Who is *that?*" I was pretty sure I've never seen the woman before.

"You know,"—Doris looked at the woman, tilting her head one way, then the other—"if I'm not mistaken, that's Fay Tality. My, oh, my. I haven't seen her in years. She took off straight after her eighteenth birthday, and that must've been ten, twelve years ago."

"She's done some growing up since then."

"Right?" Doris mimed grabbing her boobs. "Especially her ta-tas. Do you think they're real?"

I snorted. "Dunno." Fay's chest was certainly well-endowed, spilling over the top of her black halter neck. She sported a full tattoo sleeve on one arm, along with half a dozen bracelets. She wore skintight black jeans and stilettoes, and with her peroxide blonde hair falling in soft waves around her shoulders and her bright red lipstick and winged eyeliner, she could've stepped straight off the pages of an edgy magazine. Reaching up to touch my hair hastily scraped together in a messy bun, I couldn't recall the last time I'd brushed it. For sure, it had to have been this week.

I watched as the curvaceous blonde wove her way around the tables, coming to a stop at one at the back and leaning down to speak with the sole male occupant.

Dragging my eyes off Fay, I focused on the man. I'd never seen him before, but from where I was standing, he looked to be late thirties. A light stubble dusted his square jaw, but with the baseball cap he was wearing pulled low over his eyes, I couldn't make out the rest of his features.

I sucked in my breath on a hiss and grabbed Doris's arm. "Do you think it's a coincidence that Fay returns to town and Dino turns up dead? Do you think she's with the Tarkaths too? Maybe she's an assassin!"

To see his body in the rotunda had been an unexpected and unwelcome surprise. Dino was a member of the Tarkath Syndicate, an organization much like the human mafia, only the Tarkaths dealt in magic, mostly black, and I suspected they were behind the tainted wand shipment I'd stumbled upon. That little find had landed me here, hiding out and undercover in Gravestone, Texas.

"Holly Day, not like you to jump to conclusions." Doris pried my fingers from her arm. "Come on, let's grab a seat. I'm curious what those two are up to."

We took our usual table near the window,

picking up our menus to hide behind as we watched the couple.

"Tell me about Fay Tality," I invited, watching the curvaceous blonde flirting with the man. She was leaning into him, running her hands up his chest, blood-red nails impossibly long as they smoothed the fabric of his shirt. Was this a romantic liaison? Or business? For while Fay was flirting up a storm, the man remained unmoved, watching her with a smirk on his face, not encouraging her but not rebuffing her, either.

"Like I said, Fay used to live here with her grandparents. As soon as she turned eighteen, she was gone, never to return. Didn't even turn up for Marv and Henrietta's funerals." She sniffed in disapproval. "She must do all right for herself though. Those heels are Louboutin, and I'm pretty sure the jeans are Dolce and Gabbana."

I whistled through my teeth. Expensive. And out of place in Gravestone, which led me straight back to the question of why she'd returned. Did she know Dino? Did she come here to meet with him? Or was he in town to visit the mayor? Had one of them killed him?

"What do you think Dino was doing back here? I

thought he'd left when the sheriff went all bear assed on him," Doris said, reading my mind.

I smirked. "The sheriff didn't go bear assed. He went bear. Full stop."

"I wish I'd seen it." She sighed. "I bet it was a sight to behold."

The sight of Joshua Calder, aka the sheriff, striding away after he'd shifted back into human form, buck naked, flashed into my mind. Oh, yes. He'd been a sight to behold all right. Only of course I hadn't known he was a bear shifter when he'd broken down the front door and come roaring into my house, all black grizzly with gleaming teeth and flashing claws. I'd thought I was toast. That's when Dino had thrown the knife, missed the bear, and gotten me instead. My hand automatically rubbed at the fresh scar on my shoulder.

"Earth to Holly," Doris teased, dragging me out of my daydream of Calder's bare butt.

"Sorry. What?"

"I said, do you think they're here for the treasure hunt?"

And that's when things clicked into place. "Of course!" I declared, dropping the menu onto the table. "It makes perfect sense."

"It does?" Doris looked at me like I'd lost my marbles.

"Yes." I nodded, leaning in and lowering my voice. "Whatever Kerris is up to, Dino was involved. She invites everyone to a special meeting the same day Dino returns to town. That's not a coincidence. She wanted us all in one place for a reason." Even as I said it out loud, I was pretty sure I knew what that reason was. "She wanted us—*me*—out of my house."

Doris gasped. "You think she killed Dino?"

"What?" I frowned. "No. I think Kerris was as shocked as everyone else when Calder announced his death. I think Dino was intending to use the treasure hunt as a ruse, a cover."

"For what?"

I ticked off on my fingers. "Kerris sets up this meeting to get us all in one place at one time. Giving Dino the opportunity to break into my house. Again."

"What do you have that he wants?" Doris was genuinely puzzled.

"Aside from the soul stone that no one knows I have?" I said drolly.

"You think he knew about the soul stone?" Her voice shot up.

"Shh." I held a finger up to my lips. "No one

knows we have it. As far as everyone is concerned, the stone is with the Arzan Brotherhood. However, if Keelan Moore turns up, then yeah, we may have a problem."

Doris and I had gotten the puzzle box I'd bought from the markets open and had switched out the soul stone we'd found inside for a rock. I'd then handed the puzzle box back to Keelan, who'd threatened to rip my throat open if I didn't. He'd left town none the wiser. Now the soul stone was secured in the cedar elm tree in my backyard, cloaked to hide its magic. But how had Dino found out about it? I was pretty sure the stone was why Dino was back in town or searching my house—if, indeed, that's what he'd been intending to do if he hadn't been inconveniently murdered.

"Uh-oh," Doris whispered. I followed her gaze to where Fay Tality was on her feet and squaring off with none other than Gravestone's illustrious mayor, Kerris Jones, who'd just arrived and made a beeline for her table.

"You really have no clue who I am?" Kerris said.

"You'd think the confused looks and blank stare would have answered that for you." Fay sneered. Kerris was wearing her customary tweed suit, pearls around her neck and feet squeezed into pumps two sizes too small, her cheeks flushing red at Fay's insolence. Kerris looked… flustered. As if the sight of the younger woman had caught her unaware.

"The village called," Kerris snapped. "They'd like their idiot back. You better get going."

Ouch. Rude!

"If I threw a stick, you'd leave, right?" Fay shot back, unperturbed by Kerris's hostility.

"I'm Kerris Jones, mayor of Gravestone!" Kerris puffed out her chest with pride.

"Mayor?" Fay barked out a laugh. "Who'd you sleep with to get that job?"

Kerris flushed an even brighter red, her hands clenching into fists.

Fay didn't miss a thing. "No way!" She threw back her head and laughed, long and loud. "Oh my God, that's priceless." She held her belly, practically doubling over with laughter. "That is soooo funny. And now I need to pee."

Fay spun on her stiletto and sauntered away, heading toward the bathroom. I sighed. I wished I could walk so elegantly in heels. As it was, my walking boot kept my footwear decidedly unfashionable. Kerris stormed out of the café, her movements jerky and fueled with rage, the polar opposite of Fay.

"Well," Doris said, tossing her menu on the table. "I don't know about you, but I could use some pancakes!"

Right on cue, River turned up to take our order. "What'll it be, Holly?"

"Hey!" Doris protested. "What about me?"

River sighed and shook her head. "You'll have your usual, Doris, like you always do. Eggs and pancakes with two pieces of bacon and a caramel latte."

Doris's eyes widened. "How did you know?"

"Because it's what you always have, silly." River chuckled. The bell over the door rang, and we automatically glanced to see who'd arrived.

"Just take a seat anywhere," River called out to the newcomer. "I'll be by to take your order shortly."

A man in his early thirties, wearing tan cargo pants and a blue tee shirt, a backpack slung over one shoulder, nodded at River.

"What do you think?" I asked no one in particular. "Treasure hunter?"

"Could be," Doris agreed.

"Is that what Kerris's meeting was about this morning? That silly treasure hunt?" River asked, folding her arms. "She was really sour at me for not attending, but I have a business to run. I can't just close my doors because of a Women's Committee Meeting—sorry, ladies."

Doris waved away her apology. "You would have been sorrier if you'd come. Total waste of time. Although watching Holly toss Calder over her shoulder almost made up for it."

"You what?" River grabbed my arm, eyes like saucers.

I grinned sheepishly. "It was a self-defense demonstration, and well... I was never very good at following instructions."

"How do you know about the treasure hunt, anyway?" Doris asked, clearly done with talking about me and Calder.

River shrugged. "Well, that guy there who just came in? His name is Jensen Chapman, and he's the organizer. He was in here earlier asking if he could drop off a clue."

"You're part of the treasure hunt?"

"Not me, personally, but the café is. But you two can't tell anybody! Contestants have to work out the clues themselves, and then if they get it right, I have to stamp their card and give them the next clue. Kerris would kill me if we messed it up. You know"—she tapped her lip—"that's probably why she had y'all at the meeting. So the clues could be planted without y'all finding out about it."

Doris and I looked at each other. Could it be so simple? That Kerris had opened up the meeting to everyone to get us out of the way while the treasure hunt was set up? That it wasn't a ruse to break into my home?

"I hardly think a treasure hunt like that would attract Dino back to town," I said.

"Dino's back?" River asked, surprised.

I glanced at Doris. It seemed the gossip mill hadn't reached River's café yet. "Yeah. I found his body in the rotunda this morning."

River's eyes rounded into saucers. "He's *dead?*" she whispered.

Doris nodded. "Murdered."

"Wow. I mean... oh my... how? How do you know he was *murdered?*" She hissed the last word.

"Gaping wound in his chest tells me it wasn't natural causes." I shrugged, and her eyes bugged out even more.

"How much is the prize if it attracted the likes of Dino to participate?" Doris asked.

"Jensen told me the major prize is a hundred dollar gift voucher to Camping World," River said.

Hardly enough to bring Dino to town. Which

meant he'd come for something else. Something that got him killed.

"What about that other guy?" I jerked my head toward the man Fay had been sitting with.

"Nope, no clue who he is." River paused for a minute, looking from me to Doris and back again. "No clue? Get it?"

"Oh! Har har." Doris laughed.

"Sorry, guys, I've gotta go take Jensen's order. Do you know what you want yet, Holly?"

I ordered the same as Doris and watched as River left to attend to her other customers. Jensen Chapman was one hundred percent a stranger to me, but the other guy who'd been talking with Fay? He was strikingly familiar, yet I couldn't place him. I couldn't put my finger on where or when we'd met before, but I was certain we had.

CHAPTER FIVE

"Doris Shutt, as I live and breathe! How are you?" Fay Tality beamed at Doris, seemingly delighted to see her. Doris shot me a *what the hell* look.

"I'm doing great, Fay," Doris replied. "How about yourself? It's been a while since we've seen you in Gravestone. Truth be told, I didn't think you'd ever be back."

Fay smiled, pulled out a chair, and sat down at our table. "You don't mind if I join you, do you? My date left."

I glanced across the room and sure enough, the stranger had gone. Odd that I hadn't seen him leave, but then I'd been distracted by shoving pancakes into my mouth.

Fay turned her attention to me. "Hi, I'm Fay Tality." She smiled, red lipstick making her teeth appear whiter, her blue eyes sparkling. She was even more stunning up close.

"Holly Day." No one batted an eye at our ridiculous names. I wondered if hers was as fake as mine?

"Bring me up to speed, Fay," Doris said, taking a sip of her latte. "What have you been doing with yourself?"

Fay blew out a breath. "Gosh, where do I start? I spent the first few years after leaving Gravestone working in a tattoo parlor, learning the trade." She held out her tattooed arm. "Then, believe it or not, I got into blogging—travel and fashion—and now I'm what you'd call an influencer on social media."

"And you make money from this?" Doris's eyebrows shot up and Fay laughed.

"Oh yes, it's very lucrative."

"So what brings you back to Gravestone?" I asked. "I can't imagine there's much of a story in the upcoming treasure hunt."

Fay laughed again and reached over to pat my arm. "When you're an influencer, it's all about visibility. But you're right. Ordinarily, I wouldn't have accepted the invitation to open the treasure hunt, but when I saw it was in Gravestone… well, let's just say nostalgia took hold, and I figured why not swing by my old home town and see what's changed. Plus, it doesn't hurt my credibility that part of the proceeds go to charity."

"You have to pay to join in?" I asked. I'd never participated in a treasure hunt before. Frankly, it had zero appeal, but, as they say, different strokes for different folks.

"Yep. Twenty dollars. Jensen can tell you all about it—have you met him yet?" She swiveled in her seat to wave at Jensen several tables away.

"And your date? Who was he? Is he with the treasure hunt, too?" Doris asked.

Fay nodded. "Yes, that's Luke Bizzy. He's media liaison."

"I had no idea the treasure hunt was such a big deal," I said.

Fay laughed. "Well, it's not, not really. Luke's a freelancer. He's representing the charity. They currently have a campaign running to raise their profile, and this was a good opportunity to get their name out there."

Doris narrowed her eyes. "So, this date wasn't

really a date, was it? More of a business meeting. If he's media liaison and you're a social media influencer."

Fay threw back her head and laughed again. "You got me. You always were a sharp one, Doris Shutt. But listen"—she sobered and lowered her voice—"I overheard River telling someone that there's been a murder. And that you found the body." Her blue eyes locked on mine.

Leaning back in my chair, I crossed my arms. "I have zero interest in being plastered all over social media, thank you very much." That would be a disaster and would one hundred percent blow my cover.

"Oh no, no I'm sorry, you misunderstood my interest." Fay's apology sounded sincere. "No, the reason I'm asking, and listen ladies, this is a secret, I haven't told any of my followers this and to be perfectly honest I don't want it getting out, so rest assured, what we're talking about here isn't for social media or my blog, I promise."

"What is it?" Doris leaned in, intrigued. "What's your secret?"

"I'm studying intelligence analysis. When I pass, I'll be going to Glynco to join the Criminal

Investigator Training Program. I know, I know, I don't look like the type. I look like I'm on the fast path for a biker chick career, but looks can be deceiving, can't they?"

"I don't see why that's a secret," I said, confused. What did it matter if people knew she wanted to join the FBI?

"Once you reach a certain influencer status, your fans think you owe them, that you have an obligation to not only keep on producing the same content they've come to know and love, but that you share every little bit of your life with them. Do you know how tiresome that is? At first, it was a thrill, and I admit I initially enjoyed the fame, but this isn't a career I see myself pursuing ten years from now. Another younger, pretty face will come along and believe me, it gets stressful thinking up new ways to stay engaged, to stay current. But my following likes to think of me as a blonde airhead. It'd go down like a lead balloon if they knew that ultimately, I want to pursue a career in law enforcement."

"They're going to find out eventually," I pointed out.

"Yes, but I want to be qualified by then. And of course, I'd be closing down all of my social media accounts because I wouldn't want there to be any conflicts of interest."

Doris and I looked at each other. Could we trust her to help us? With her studies in criminology, she brought a new perspective, and possibly skill set, to the table.

"And you promise none of this—other than the treasure hunt—is going on social media? Or your blog? Or the internet in any way whatsoever?"

"I promise I won't mention a thing about it. It would go against me if my future employers saw me discussing active cases on the socials. That's another reason I don't want my followers knowing what my plans are. If this leaked, it would kill my new career before it got started."

Doris rubbed her hands together. "Well then, it sounds like we all have secrets to keep. A win-win."

Fay smiled sweetly at Doris, the smile fading when she turned back to me. "So, tell me about the body you found. Do you know the victim?"

"It was Dino Cittadino," I said.

"And he's a local? I'm not familiar with that name."

I shook my head. "Nope. Dino doesn't live here but visits from time to time. Mostly for the markets." I left out the part about being a member of the

Tarkath Syndicate. While I was prepared to take Fay at face value, I wasn't one hundred percent sure I could trust her. If I told her sensitive SIA information and it ended up on the internet... well, I suspect Scott Harding would have a conniption.

"And what about you, Holly? How long have you lived here?" Fay asked.

"I'm new. I haven't been here long at all. I inherited my great uncle's estate. John Smith."

Fay's brows rose. "You're John Smith's great niece? I didn't know he had any family. He never said."

"He and Mom were estranged." My cover story had held up so far, and Fay was no exception, accepting my explanation despite the surprise that she—or anyone—hadn't known John had any family.

"So, is it true what River said?" Fay asked.

"About what?"

"That you found the body—Dino—this morning? What were you even doing out in that weather? The rain was torrential."

I glanced out the window at the now beautiful albeit steamy day outside. Calder had been right. The storm had rolled over Gravestone in a matter of minutes. If I'd waited a short while, I could have taken my bike ride without getting soaked. Or crashing into the pothole and taking the skin off my knee and elbow.

"We should go," I said to Doris, rising and pushing my chair under the table. "We've got stuff to do."

Doris stood and Fay followed suit.

"Do you mind if I come? I really want to know more about Dino, and you haven't told me what happened." Fay's blue eyes swept over the café before returning to me. "I take it you can't talk freely here. Maybe we could go back to my hotel room?"

Goosebumps rose on my arms, and the hairs on the back of my neck stood on end.

"Pft, no need for that," Doris interjected. "We'll go back to my place. You might be able to help us with something."

"Is your place still done up for Christmas?" Fay asked, linking her arm with Doris's, the pair of them preceding me out of the café while they reminisced about Gravestone some ten odd years ago. As I trailed along behind, my walking boot thumping on the floor, I rubbed my hands over my forearms, settling the goosebumps. I didn't know why I'd reacted to Fay's invitation to join her in her hotel room in that way. All I could say was it gave me the heebie jeebies and a little alarm had gone off in my head, a warning to steer clear. Of her hotel room or Fay herself, I couldn't say.

"What is that noise? That strange thumping noise?" Fay listened, then turned, her eyes coming to rest on my walking boot. "Oh, darlin', you're hurt!"

"It's nothing." I brushed off her concern.

"What happened?"

"Broken navicular. Shouldn't need to wear this thing for much longer."

"Can't wait to get back into heels, huh?"

I eyed her five-inch stilettos that had her towering over Doris. "Yeah." Pretty sure that was a lie, but since I couldn't recall if I wore heels or not, I figured I'd go with the flow. Outside, parked next to Doris's Impala, was a sporty red convertible with the top down. Fay headed toward it.

"You're still driving the beast I see, Doris," she said, standing between the two vehicles. "Never considered something… smaller?"

"No need. She still runs, and that's all I need." Doris patted the roof of the Impala.

I cleared my throat. "We should get going."

Climbing into our respective cars, we waited for Fay to pull out first, her sports car starting with a purr before she pulled smoothly away. Doris started the Impala with a roar and shot out of our parking spot with a lot less finesse.

"Are you sure we can trust her?" I asked Doris as we sped down Main Street.

Doris shrugged. "I don't see any reason not to, do you?"

"I got an odd feeling when she mentioned going back to her hotel room," I confessed, still not sure what to make of it.

"She wasn't asking you back for a hook-up." Doris chuckled.

"I didn't think she was," I protested. "I'm just saying when she issued the invitation, I got goosebumps, and the hairs on the back of my neck stood up."

I thought Doris would laugh and tease me some more. Instead, she shot me a serious look, her face thoughtful. "Interesting. We'll keep an eye on her. Anyway, I figured she could help us with the phone."

"Dino's phone?" My voice went up three octaves, and I had to clear my throat. "You're going to trust her with the fact that I stole evidence from a crime scene?"

"If we want the phone unlocked, then we're going to have to crack a few eggs. And I figure someone of

Fay's generation—plus with her social media smarts —might know a thing or two about cell phones."

"You realize that will give away the fact that we're investigating Dino's murder?"

"I know. And that's exactly what Fay is going to do. Come on, put two and two together, Holly. Fay wants to join the FBI, become a federal agent. And here she is, in her hometown, presented with a murder. You can bet your bottom socks she's going to be sticking her nose in and putting her studies to good use. Better to have her working with us where we can keep an eye on her."

Doris had a point. From the little I knew about Fay Tality, there was no way she wouldn't investigate Dino's murder. Even if it was for her blog or socials or whatever, she was going to poke around, and if she poked in the wrong place with the wrong stick, she just might find herself hurt. She didn't know what we did, that Dino was a member of the Tarkaths. It wouldn't be long before they sent someone to avenge his death, and if they found Fay sniffing around, they may very well decide that she needed taking out. And I don't mean on a date.

"Keep your friends close and your enemies closer," I said out loud.

"Fay's not our enemy, Holly," Doris said. "She's our friend."

"I thought you didn't like her. You sounded mad about her not coming home for her grandparents' funerals."

Doris lifted a shoulder in a half shrug. "Just cos I'm mad doesn't mean I don't like her. I'm guessing she had her reasons. In the meantime, let's find out who killed Dino Cittadino."

CHAPTER SIX

F ay didn't bat a fake eyelash when Doris handed her Dino's phone and said, "Have a go at unlocking that for us, love."

Taking the phone, Fay headed into the living room, making herself comfortable on the sofa, legs up, with the phone in her face and her thumbs moving across the screen.

"While she does that, let's take another look at that powder," Doris said, grabbing a microscope from under the kitchen sink and thumping it down on the table.

I pulled the treasure hunt flyer from my back pocket and carefully unfolded it. Each time I did so, we lost more powder, and if we didn't identify it soon, we'd have nothing left to work with.

Using a butter knife, I scooped a tiny portion of the red substance onto a glass slide and slid it under the microscope. Bending low, I peered through the lens.

"Anything?" Doris asked, standing next to me.

I leaned back and looked at her. "I don't know who I'm kidding," I confessed. "I have no idea what I'm looking at, and if I did, I can't remember it."

"Scootch over," she instructed. "Let me try."

"So, Holly," Fay called from the living room. "You never finished telling me about finding Dino's body."

"Go ahead," Doris said. "Fill her in. I'm going to study this for a bit." Doris had a notebook by her side and was jotting down notes on what she could see through the microscope. "We may swing by the library later and look at their chemistry books."

Joining Fay in the living room, I sank onto one of the armchairs by the window and repeated what I'd already told Calder and Doris. An early morning bike ride in the rain had resulted in me discovering Dino's lifeless corpse in the rotunda. Missing his heart.

"How exciting." Fay shot me a look over the top of Dino's phone before returning her attention to the screen.

"That's one word for it, I guess."

"Was there anything else? At the crime scene, I mean. Any clues? Smart of you to swipe the phone, by the way. The cops would have to do this through official channels, with warrants and requests to service providers. Much faster to crack the phone and find out exactly what Dino was up to, who he saw, who he was communicating with."

"Yeah, that's what I thought too."

"So?" Fay prompted.

"What?"

"Any other clues? What's Doris working on?"

"I found a substance on the body that may or may not be relevant. I took a little sample. Doris is trying to identify it." I didn't mention the treasure hunt flyer clutched in his hand, nor the symbol carved into his palm. While Doris was all in with trusting Fay, I needed more time to get there. Not to mention Fay was human. She'd immediately jump to some sort of conclusion about the occult items, like Dino's death being a satanic ritual, which I was certain it was not.

"Cool," Fay murmured without looking up.

"How's it going with the phone?" I asked.

"I think I've almost got it."

"How do you do that, anyway? Unlock a locked cell phone?"

"I did a couple of semesters in cyber security," Fay said. "We learned a few things, and one of them was all about coding. Basically, all our technology is built on code. And that's how hackers get into your computer and steal your data, by using code."

"So that's what you're doing? Writing code?"

"Sort of. A bunch of students developed a hack. It's not part of the official syllabus because, you know, hacking is frowned upon, but I kept the code on a note app on my phone—never know when it might come in handy."

"Like now."

"Exactly like now!" She sat upright, waving the phone in the air. "I did it! I'm in!"

"Really?"

"Yup."

I got up and moved to sit next to her on the sofa, both our heads bent over Dino's phone as Fay brought up Dino's call list.

"Last person Dino called was Kerris Jones. Your mayor," Fay said. "What's the mayor doing taking calls from the likes of Dino Cittadino?"

"What do you mean, the likes of Dino Cittadino? I thought you didn't know him?"

Fay shot me an exasperated look. "I don't *know* him, but I know *of* him. He runs with the Tarkaths, from what I've heard. He's been visiting Gravestone on and off for years. I remember Marv and Henrietta had dealings with him a time or two."

"Really?" I sat up straight. I was intrigued that Fay knew about the Tarkaths and made a mental note to tell Doris later. Not to mention that, earlier, Fay had acted like she didn't know Dino at all, that he was a total stranger to her. "What sort of dealings?"

"Just selling a few old antiques when they were hard up for cash. They used to have a stall at the markets. Dino became somewhat of a regular. What do you make of him calling the mayor late at night?"

I flopped back in my chair. "They had a thing."

"A thing?"

"You know." I shot her a hard look. "A thing. Romantic liaison."

"Oh! That type of thing." She paused to think it over. "I'm not sure if I should be impressed or grossed out."

"Exactly." I sighed, tilting my head back and gazing up at the ceiling. "So Dino called Kerris. What time?"

"Ten forty-seven. A booty call?"

If Kerris Jones had gotten some loving last night, it certainly hadn't changed her demeanor today.

"Any other calls?" I asked.

"Yeah, but I don't recognize any of the numbers. They're not saved as contacts."

"Texts?"

Fay was silent while she scanned through Dino's text messages. "Several between Dino and Jensen Chapman discussing sponsorship of the treasure hunt. Boring." She made a snoring noise. "Wait a second... what do we have here?"

"What is it?"

"Messages between Dino and Luke Bizzy."

"Your friend, Luke Bizzy?" The man Fay had been flirting with at River's. The same man who was vaguely familiar.

"Acquaintance," she clarified. "Listen to this! Dino says,"

Do you have it?

Price has gone up.

That wasn't the deal.

10k or I take it to another buyer.

My boss isn't going to be happy.

Not my concern. 2 am at the rotunda.

"And?" I prompted when Fay stopped reading. "What did Dino say?"

"Nothing. He didn't reply to the last text."

"Check the call log immediately after the messages from Luke. Did Dino call his boss?"

"He made a few calls but not immediately after the messages from Luke. And the calls he made aren't saved as contacts, so I'm thinking not his boss."

I headed to the dining room to fill Doris in, only to find her in the kitchen.

"Any luck?" I asked, jerking my head toward the remaining red powder on the table. The microscope was gone.

She shook her head. "Maybe. I'm going to the library to do some research. But first, coffee! How did you two get on? Get the phone unlocked?"

"Yes!" Fay appeared behind me, making me jump. I hadn't heard her approach and thought she was still reclining on the sofa. "Remember that guy I was talking to in the café earlier? Luke? Get this." Her voice was laced with excitement as she told Doris what we'd discovered.

Doris's excitement matched Fay's. "We've got him! We've got our killer!"

"Hold on, we don't know that," I cautioned,

although to be fair, it looked suspect that Luke had arranged to meet Dino at the rotunda at two in the morning. It wasn't a stretch to think he'd killed him.

"Come on, Holly, it's not rocket surgery," Doris whined, scrunching up her face in a frown. "Why else would Luke meet Dino at that hour of the morning if not for murder?"

Ignoring Doris's mixed metaphor, I said, "Are you forgetting Dino also buys antiquities and occult objects? Luke may have been arranging a legitimate sale." I mean, I doubted it, yet I felt compelled to play the devil's advocate.

"Here." Doris shoved a coffee cup into my hand and pointed me toward the dining room. Doris and Fay were following with their own drinks when the unthinkable happened. Doris took her seat, but as Fay approached the table, her toe caught on the rug and she tripped, her coffee spilling over the tabletop.

"Oh, no!" Fay cried. "I'm so sorry. Are you all right, Doris? You didn't get burned, did you? Oh gosh, I'm sorry, it's these stupid heels. They got caught on the rug."

Doris pushed back her chair and gave herself a pat down. "I'm fine, I'm fine. The coffee didn't get me. Can't say the same for our evidence, though."

The flyer was awash with coffee, the powder obliterated, our evidence gone.

"I'll get some paper towel." Hurrying back into the kitchen, I grabbed the roll Doris kept above the sink and began tearing off strips, laying it on the dining table to soak up the piping hot coffee.

"Do you think it's ruined the table?" Fay hovered, watching. "Doris, I'm so sorry. I'll get you a new dining table."

Doris waved away her offer. "Nonsense. It'll be fine. Nothing a little polish can't fix."

"I'm sorry." Fay sounded like she was about to cry.

"Stop apologizing, child. It was an accident, not your fault. I was pretty much done with the powder, anyway."

Fay's head snapped up. "You were? Oh, that's a relief! So, you *did* find out what it was?"

"I think it's some sort of striking powder."

"Striking powder?" I asked. "What's that?"

"Something gardeners use to get off cuts to take root. They dip it in the striking powder before planting to encourage new root growth."

"Interesting." Any resident of Gravestone probably had striking powder in their garden shed, which didn't narrow our pool of suspects down at all. In fact, the only suspect I had was Luke Bizzy. Although I shouldn't cross Kerris Jones off the list. Maybe Dino had ended their relationship, and she'd killed him in the heat of the moment, then set it up to look like a ritualistic killing to hide her tracks. Implausible but not impossible.

"So, what's next?" Fay called from the kitchen, where she was fixing another cup of coffee.

I shot Doris a look. "Are you sure she can be trusted?" I hissed.

"Of course. She's Henrietta and Marv's granddaughter. One of us."

"Us? As in *witch?*"

Doris frowned at me. "No, silly. Us as in a citizen of Gravestone."

"She's been gone for ten years."

"Doesn't matter."

"So once the locals deem you a local, it sticks. Forever?"

"Actually," Fay said. "I was born here. So yeah, I qualify as a local."

Oops. I didn't realize she'd returned and was now standing behind me. The woman sure was silent on her Louboutin heels.

"What about your parents? Where are they?" I

figured since we were already getting personal, it couldn't hurt to ask.

Fay took a seat, cradling her coffee between her palms, her blue eyes direct. "My mom died in childbirth. I never knew who my father was. Neither did my grandparents, Henrietta and Marv, who raised me."

"And yet you left town as soon as you turned eighteen. Why's that?"

Fay let out a tinkling laugh. "Hello? Have you seen Gravestone? It's a one-horse town if ever I've seen one. I wanted… more. More adventure, more excitement, more opportunities. And you can't get around the massive generational gap between me and my grandparents. Don't get me wrong, I appreciate everything they did for me. If it weren't for them, I'd have been in the foster system, so I'm grateful they gave me a home. But that came with conditions. Like control." She raised both shoulders in a shrug. "Turns out I don't respond well to being controlled by others. Enough about me. Tell me about you, Holly. I didn't know John Smith had any family."

Good job of turning the tables, Fay. I hid my smirk behind my coffee cup.

"Not much to tell. Like you, I lost my mom

young, however I had no family—that I was aware of —to take me in, so I ended up in the foster system. I didn't know about John Smith until the lawyers eventually tracked me down to tell me I'd inherited his estate. Such as it is."

"And your foot? How did you do that?" She nodded toward my walking boot tucked under the table.

Funny thing, after all my time in Gravestone, no one had actually asked me that question. Meeting Fay's gaze head on, I shrugged. "Rolled it. Much like you'd sprain your ankle, only I fractured a bone instead."

"Sounds painful." She made the appropriate noises of sympathy, which I waved away, hiding behind my cup once more. A headache was beginning to twinge behind my eyes, and I absently rubbed at my temple while my mind drifted to Dino Cittadino. Doris had pursued the red powder clue with gusto, and Fay had cracked his phone, so we now knew who Dino had been communicating with. While it appeared Luke Bizzy was definitely a suspect, I needed more than a text message before declaring him guilty. But there were two clues left unexplored, and they just might give me the irrefutable proof I needed.

The treasure hunt flyer clenched in his hand and the symbol carved into his palm. Both of which I had no intention of sharing with Fay. Not yet, anyway. I had more at stake than Doris, and if Fay found out the truth about me, well, let's just say I wasn't convinced she'd be able to keep the news to herself. Despite her apparent training in criminology, she was still a blogger and a social media influencer, both of which involved sharing her life with the public. If Fay discovered I was an SIA agent hiding out in Gravestone? I suspected that juicy morsel would be too good *not* to share.

"Everything okay, Holly?" Doris asked. "You look a little peaky."

I figured I looked as wrung out as I felt. "Bit of a headache is all," I confessed. "It's been a long day."

"You didn't give yourself a concussion, did you? When you came off the bike?"

"What? No! Don't be ridiculous, that was hours ago, and anyway, I didn't hit my head."

"Come on, I'll give you a lift home." Doris was on her feet, reaching for her keys, when Fay stopped her.

"No need. I have to head off, anyway. I have a date. I'll drop Holly home."

"You have a date?" Doris lit up like the Christmas tree in the living room corner. "Who with?"

Fay winked. "Well, now, that would be telling, wouldn't it?"

"Duh, of course it would. So, come on, spill. Who's your date with?"

"Actually, it's quite timely, considering… my date is with Luke Bizzy."

"No way!" Doris's mouth hung open like she was catching flies before she snapped it shut and frowned. "Fay," she cautioned. "That could be dangerous. He's a killer."

"Don't worry, I know how to handle myself. I'll be perfectly safe. Anyway, that little text message isn't enough to convince a jury that he's a killer— and even if he is, I'm betting Luke's smart enough to get himself an alibi for the time of death. So, I'm going to keep my date because, let's face it, the man is gorgeous, and I'm going to do a little digging while I'm at it, see what I can find out about him."

Doris looked at me, and I shrugged. Had to admit, if it were me, I'd keep the date too. "Keep us posted," I said, not sure what to make of Fay Tality.

CHAPTER SEVEN

"You're sure no one has been here today? Were you here the entire time?" Fay had dropped me at home just as the sun set and the moon rose majestically over the mangroves. I'd had no idea it was that late. The day had really gotten away from me.

Flynn stood on his back legs, planted his fists on his little rat hips, and glared at me. Doris and I had dropped him back home right before the Women's Committee Meeting this morning, meaning he would have been here had someone attempted to gain entry while I was busy elsewhere.

"It wouldn't be the first time someone has broken in without you being aware of it," I grumbled, tossing my bag onto the foot of the camping cot in the living room, my temporary bedroom. John's possessions had been… let's just say less than sanitary, and I'd carted almost everything to the dump. Except for a couple of bookcases and the kitchen table, the house had been stripped. Which was why I found it odd that people kept breaking in. There was nothing left to steal. Nevertheless, I couldn't shake the feeling someone had been in the house during my absence.

Despite Flynn assuring me no one had broken in, I cased the house, going from room to room, searching for signs of an intruder. I found none.

"I know what you're thinking." I eyeballed the furry rodent. "How could Dino break in here if he was already dead? Yeah, well, obviously, I meant they sent someone else in his place. Maybe even the person who killed him. Kerris is up to something," I said to Flynn. "I just know it. Take her reaction when Calder announced Dino's murder. She'd initially been shocked, but then she shut down. And she did not tell Calder about the phone call with Dino last night—which I assume led to them hooking up. So, technically, she's withholding information from the police, only I can't very well hand over the evidence to prove it."

"And why gather us all together like she did if not

to get me out of the way? Maybe Casey told her about the book he found in the wall, and she hired Dino to get it. Do her dirty work? It wouldn't be the first time."

Flynn sat on the kitchen counter watching me. The book was the only thing—other than the soul stone—that was remotely interesting about this house. Unless John Smith had other secrets hidden within the walls, which was entirely possible. I was starting to realize there was a lot more to the man than met the eye.

Flynn squeaked and waved his paws around. It would be so much easier if I could understand him, although we'd worked out a way to communicate, of sorts. He would type on my laptop, and although it was slow and tedious, it worked. But rather than heading toward the laptop, Flynn jumped from the counter and headed for the canvas backpack where I'd tossed it onto the cot when I'd come in.

Watching him through the framework of the partly demolished wall that Dino and I had crashed through the last time he'd broken in, I rolled my eyes, crossed my arms, and waited, wondering how long it would take Flynn to ask for my help as he tried to drag the book we'd found out of my bag. The answer was one minute, twelve seconds.

Huffing and puffing, he finally stopped and glared at me.

"Need a hand?" Sarcasm rolled off my tongue.

He nodded, and I retrieved the book, taking it to the kitchen table. The book itself was old, bound in leather with a cord wrapped around it. Etched into the cover were occult symbols, and on the pages inside were notes, spells, lists of names, and sketches. I'd initially thought the book to be a grimoire, a witch's journal, but it was so much more than that. The handwriting changed several times, showing it had changed ownership over the years. John Smith had been the last one to own it, and he was now dead.

Leaving Flynn to pore over the journal, I fixed myself a sandwich, pondering over the origins of the book and if it was, in fact, related to Dino's death at all. Was the book what Dino had been searching for when he broke in the last time? He'd gained access via the upstairs bedroom window, which was an odd entry point. The only thing in that room was an old bookcase, which was what made me think Dino was looking for a book. And not any book. The old journal John Smith had had the foresight to hide.

"I wonder who else knew about it," I said, pouring a fresh cup of coffee. Flynn didn't reply, and when I turned around, the reason became apparent. He was sound asleep, spread eagle on his back in the middle of the book. "Sleeping on the job… again?" Shaking my head, I sat down, sliding him off the book and onto the tabletop, where he continued to snore his little head off.

"What *were* you up to, Dino Cittadino?" It was a rhetorical question, so when the lights suddenly went out, I jumped, spilling my coffee in my lap. With a hiss, I leaped to my feet and rushed to the sink. Grabbing a dishcloth, I wiped away the scalding coffee, wincing as the cloth scraped over burned skin. "Darn it," I cursed. "That hurt."

The only light in the room was moonlight filtering through the kitchen window. I could just make out the shape of Flynn, who'd woken at my cursing and was now upright, ears swiveling.

"I'm okay," I reassured him. "Spilled my coffee when the lights went out." As suddenly as the lights had gone out, they came back on again. Flynn and I looked at each other. "Weird, huh?" I said. "Must be some sort of fluctuation in the power grid."

Flynn didn't look convinced. Although, to be fair, he was a rat. He had limited facial expressions. My headache from earlier amplified in intensity, a sharp, stabbing pain behind my left eyeball that had me wincing. My stomach churned and my head spun. Sweat beaded on my skin, and that awful clammy feeling just before you hurl swept over me.

"I don't feel so good," I muttered, heading for the staircase, staggering as the room dipped and swayed with each movement, bile crawling up my throat. At the foot of the stairs, I collapsed onto my hands and knees. Sweat beaded on my skin as I battled the nausea and pain pounding through my brain.

Flynn started squeaking, but I couldn't even look at him. Instead, I made my way upstairs to the bathroom in an undignified crawl, hanging my head over the toilet bowl and puking up the sandwich I'd eaten earlier. After what felt like hours but was probably only minutes, I sat back, leaning against the cool tile of the wall, and closed my eyes.

Flynn climbed onto my thigh.

"I dunno," I answered his unspoken question. "But I feel like death. I've got the worst headache. Do you think you can get me some Advil? There's some in my backpack."

He scampered away, and I slipped into semi-consciousness. While my stomach had stopped spasming, I still felt nauseated, and my head was killing me, like someone had a knife and was repeatedly stabbing me through the eye and into my brain. Was I having an embolism? A stroke?

I must have been drifting in and out, for the next thing I knew, Calder was by my side, sliding one hand around the nape of my neck, the other under my chin and raising my face. I opened my eyes just enough to squint at him.

"Hey there," he said softly. "What's going on?"

"Oh, you know." I groaned. "I wanted to get a better look at the floor tiles."

"Right. Flynn tells me you're not well."

It was too much of an effort to even attempt to keep my eyes open, so I closed them, only slightly annoyed that I didn't get to look at Calder's handsome face anymore. "Flynn talks too much." I didn't even know Flynn had left the house. I'd asked him to get me Advil, not the sheriff.

"Come on, let's get you off the floor." Calder scooped me into his arms and carried me downstairs as if I weighed nothing. It would have been romantic if I wasn't sweating like a pig and trying desperately not to vomit on him. Laying me on the cot, he crouched by my side and lay a palm on my forehead. "You're burning up."

"Thank you."

He chuckled, removing his hand. "I'm going to get you some water."

"And Advil," I groaned.

"And Advil," he repeated.

"I'll wait here."

"You do that."

He was back within seconds. I was drifting in and out of some sort of fugue state, barely conscious, silently terrified that something bad was happening to me. Was I about to die? Was my brain about to leak out of my ears?

Calder eased me upward, holding a glass to my lips.

"Open," he commanded. I did. He shoved two pills into my mouth, then tilted the glass. "Swallow."

"What are you doing here, anyway?" I mumbled as he lay me back down.

"Flynn got me."

"But why? Why do you even care?"

Shifting to sit on the floor next to the cot, the humor in his voice was unmistakable. "Maybe it's because you're a hotheaded, insanely independent pain in my rear woman who blew into town and wedged herself firmly under my skin."

"Like a splinter," I whispered, lulled by the timber

of his voice. I could lay there and listen to him talk for hours.

"Not quite like a splinter." He was silent for a moment, then added, "But close."

He may have said something else. I wasn't sure, for as much as I tried to hold on and stay awake and somewhat aware, it was impossible, and I slipped into oblivion, comforted by his presence.

CHAPTER EIGHT

I woke to the sounds of rain hammering the roof and thunder rumbling overhead and the scent of bacon. Disorientated, I sat up. I didn't remember coming to bed, and why on earth did I sleep in my clothes?

"Morning," Calder called from the kitchen. "How are you feeling?"

"What—" I croaked, clearing my throat before trying again. "What are you doing here?"

His face appeared in the framework of the broken wall. "You don't remember?"

I pinched the bridge of my nose and screwed my eyes shut. I felt hungover. "Did Doris and I get into the hooch last night?"

"Not that I'm aware of." He disappeared from view. "Come on. Breakfast is ready."

Climbing out of bed, I hobbled to join him. Calder looked right at home in my kitchen, wearing jeans and a T-shirt, feet bare as he plated up bacon and eggs. A fresh mug of coffee sat steaming on the table.

"Sit," he ordered. I did, thoroughly confused about why he was here, and why he was cooking breakfast. Did we…? I glanced down at my fully clothed body, not sure whether to be relieved at the realization that he was not here on a booty call. I most definitely wouldn't be fully clothed if that were the case.

Calder placed a plate of food in front of me. "I repeat, how are you feeling?" He took the seat opposite, digging into his breakfast.

"A little rough, but okay, I guess." I followed suit, shoving bacon into my mouth. I hadn't realized I was hungry until that first mouthful, then I couldn't get enough, shoveling the food in when I'd barely swallowed.

"Easy there." Calder watched me, an intrigued expression on his face. "Don't choke."

I felt a flush of embarrassment heat my cheeks. "Sorry."

He waved his fork at me. "Don't apologize for having a healthy appetite. Nothing wrong with enjoying your food. Just don't forget to chew."

After finishing my meal, I sat the knife and fork neatly across my plate and picked up my coffee, cradling the cup in my hands. "Please tell me what happened last night."

"You don't remember?"

I rolled my eyes. "Can we not do this again? The whole answer a question with a question thing because surely you know by now that I find it immensely irritating. No. I don't remember. And before you ask me what I *do* remember, it's this. Flynn and I were here. I made sandwiches for dinner because I'd had a big lunch and wasn't very hungry. Then I got the world's worst headache. I remember crawling to the bathroom, puking, and that's pretty much it." I leveled my gaze at him. "Your turn. Why are you here?"

"I'm here because Flynn turned up at my place. Flynn only turns up when you're in trouble, so I figured you needed help. I found you slumped in the bathroom, clearly unwell. Figured you triggered your allergy."

I blinked, wondering what on earth he was talking about when I remembered the lie I'd told him to cover up the time I'd touched the hexed stone that had killed Seth Saltzman. I'd told Calder I was allergic to certain dust like pathogens. The reality had been I'd caught the tail end of the hex and it had felt like I'd been dipped in acid. Last night's pain was different.

"You think it was my allergy?"

He shrugged. "Seems plausible. You kept complaining of a headache and you were vomiting. What else could it be?"

I chewed my lip, fighting an almost uncontrollable urge to tell him *everything*. That I'd taken Dino's phone and found out about his dealings with Luke Bizzy. And his call with the mayor. But most of all, I wanted to tell him I had *feelings*. That he meant something special to me and it felt all kinds of wrong to be lying to him about my entire made-up life. That was no way to start a relationship, if that was even what this was. Gravestone was having a strange effect on me. Making me softer. Making me forget things I should remember, things that I knew were buried in my brain, tantalizingly just out of reach.

"Holly?" he prompted at my hesitation.

I opened my mouth, but the words wouldn't come out. I wanted to tell him about my messed up mind, my forgotten memories. That Flynn wasn't a rat but a person. I wanted to tell him I was an SIA agent in hiding, but I was worried I'd been found out. I wanted to tell him I had a niggling suspicion Dino's death was somehow related to me.

"Nothing." I shrugged and took a sip of coffee, hiding behind the mug, but not before catching the look of disappointment that flashed across his face. "How's the investigation going?" I deflected.

"I can't talk about an ongoing case." Calder stood and carried the dirty dishes to the sink.

"Leave them. I'll do it. It's the least I can do since you cooked." I made the offer but no move to stand. I'd do it later. After he'd gone. As it was, while my headache was gone, I felt kinda hungover. Fuzzy.

"I don't mind." Filling the sink with suds, he got busy with the dishes and there was something about a barefoot man doing domestic duties that got my heart racing. I fanned my suddenly overheated cheeks and blurted, "Shouldn't you be at work?" Anything to get him out of here before I embarrassed myself.

"Dino's body is with the coroner. Deputy Biden is door-knocking and conducting inquiries in the area. Not a lot to go on until his autopsy comes back," Calder said, looking out the back window as he washed the dishes. The rain was easing. Soon it would stop altogether and the heat of the dawning day would quickly evaporate the moisture, cranking the humidity up to a thousand percent.

"You have to agree it's foul play, though, right? I mean, that wound in his chest wasn't natural causes or self-inflicted."

"Obviously," he said, sarcastically.

I eased to my feet, carrying my cup to the sink. "In that case, you should probably go relieve her. Poor woman must be exhausted."

"You'd think so, wouldn't you?" Calder muttered, half under his breath but loud enough for me to hear. "That woman has the constitution of an energizer bunny. She's a four hours a night person, if that."

"Sickening," I joked. I used to get by on six hours of sleep. These days, it was a solid eight, preferably nine. Calder turned and took the cup from me, his wet fingers brushing my skin, making me shiver. He paused. "You know, I could be forgiven for thinking you want to get rid of me," he murmured, voice deep and low. My eyes shot up to his face and what I saw there had me melting inside. Heat. Desire.

"Calder." It came out all breathless and needy, not the tough SIA agent persona I was trying so hard to cling to. *This* was not part of the brief, no matter how much my heart was telling me otherwise.

"Mmmm?" He moved without appearing to move. One minute, he was washing the dishes, the next, he was kissing me.

He tasted like bacon and coffee and fire. The kind of fire I craved. The heat of his mouth inflamed me, and his tongue sent quakes of delight shuddering through my body. My heart beat so hard and so fast, blood rushed in my ears, the roar drowning out everything around us.

After the longest, most sensual minute of my life, Calder pulled away, resting his forehead against mine, chest heaving beneath my palms.

"Why did you do that?" I whispered, shaken to my very toes. Toes that were currently curling on the linoleum floor.

"I've been wanting to do that since I first laid eyes on you," he admitted. "But you were a bristly little thing. You'd have probably had me in a headlock the second I tried it."

I chuckled. He was right. That sounded like something I would do.

"Look." Calder released me, stepping back while looking at his watch. "I do need to go. It's going to be a crazy day with the treasure hunters, not to mention a murder investigation. Are we okay?"

His question surprised me. "Er… sure?"

"I'll call you."

Wait. That sounded suspiciously like what a date would say. Were we dating now? Were we suddenly *a thing*?

"But in the meantime"—he cupped my face, his eyes intent as he lowered his head toward me, his mouth stopping tantalizingly close to mine—"do not go sticking your nose into my investigation."

"What?" I whispered, mind adrift, lost in a fog of lust at the thought of kissing him again. But I didn't get the passion filled kiss I was hoping for. I got a measly peck on the mouth and a chuckle.

"I said no poking your nose into Dino's murder. Let me do my job."

And then he was gone, leaving me standing in my kitchen, head spinning at what had just occurred. The tentative touch of Flynn's paw on my foot drew my attention.

"What?"

Flynn squeaked and waved his paws around and made a ruckus, of which I understood nothing.

"You know what?" I said. "I'm going to forget about all of this." I pointed from me to Flynn and then whirled my finger to indicate the entire house. "And we're going to focus on who killed Dino Cittadino." Which was exactly what Calder had asked me *not* to do. He should know me better by now.

Flynn squeaked and gave a curt nod, which I took to be agreement. Sitting at the kitchen table, I reached for John Smith's journal, fingers freezing as they landed on the cover. "We left this out," I whispered.

Flynn shrugged in a *so what* gesture.

"We left this out, and Calder was here. He could have seen it. I left it open on the table, I'm sure of it." Yet now it was closed and pushed to one side, partially covered beneath a dish cloth.

Flynn sat on my laptop, thumping it with his back leg.

"Okay, okay, move so I can open it." I waited for him to jump off the laptop before lifting the lid and turning it on. Once it had booted up, Flynn was all over the keyboard like he was dancing an Irish jig. Eventually, he stopped, and I leaned closer to read what he'd written.

"You can trust him."

"Really? It took you all that time just to write that?"

Flynn pointed to his short legs, then the keyboard, then the screen.

"Okay, okay, I get it. It's not easy typing with your feet."

He ran back onto the keyboard and typed some more.

"Stop worrying. Focus on the case."

"You know what? That's the best idea you've had all day." Pushing the laptop aside, I picked up the journal and began flipping through the pages. I was hunting for the rune that had been carved into Dino's palm. The same rune that had been used to kill John Smith and Seth Saltzman. Only their hearts hadn't been torn from their chests. This was different, and I needed to find out why. Maybe the rune *wasn't* the same as the ones used to kill John and Seth. Maybe I remembered it wrong. Maybe it was similar and at first glance I'd mistakenly thought them to be one and the same?

My mind drifted from the rune to the traces of red powder on Dino's chest. "Doris said she thought the powder was used in gardening, for encouraging shoots to put down roots." I paused and looked at Flynn, who was listening intently. "I'm not sure I believe that." Putting the book down, I tugged the laptop toward me, pulling up a search window.

"Why would someone use blood magic then use a non-magical item like striking powder in a ritualistic killing?"

Flynn shrugged.

"They wouldn't," I continued, pointing to the search results. "Look. None of those powders are red. They're all white. I don't think the powder is striking powder at all, so either Doris got it wrong, or she lied."

CHAPTER NINE

"Look, I'm sorry. This house is not part of the treasure hunt, and I have no clues for you."

The couple in front of me looked at each other, the map in their hands, then back at me.

"Are you sure—" the woman began, lifting the map and stabbing at it with her finger, while the man, her husband I assumed, for they wore wedding bands and kept finishing each other's sentences.

"—because the previous clue led us here," he said.

"Well, you got it wrong. Goodbye." Slamming the door, I leaned back against it, screwing my eyes shut as irritation crawled over my skin, making my magic prickle. This was the third time someone had knocked on my door, demanding I stamp their card and give them the next clue. Only I had no clue. About anything.

"Today has been the craziest day," I said to Flynn, glorious with the light behind him, his green fur appearing to glow.

Outside, I heard voices and cautiously peered out the window. The couple I'd just turned away stood on the street, speaking with a small gathering of treasure hunters who'd just arrived, and they were all looking at my house.

"Why do they think we're involved in the treasure hunt?" I asked Flynn, who shrugged and scampered into the kitchen. I followed, deciding more coffee was in order while I tried to make sense of this nonsense. Waiting for the pot to brew, I absently rubbed my fingers over the protection rune on my collarbone before stretching my arms over my head and leaning first one way, then the other, enjoying the stretch. I promised myself that once this walking boot was off, I'd get back into training and try to shed the pounds I was rapidly gaining.

I'd just straightened when I heard it. A crash, coming from the direction of my garage. As I limped to the back door, I cast a glance through the front window, not seeing the treasure hunters who'd been there moments earlier. Sure enough, I found them in my garage.

"What on earth do you think you're doing?" I demanded, standing in the open doorway. Seven treasure hunters froze. One of them, the ringleader, strode up to me, map in hand, face flushed.

"Listen, lady, you're one of the clues. We assume since you won't give us the next one that we have to find it ourselves."

"By trespassing?"

He shrugged. "Whatever it takes."

I held out a hand in a *give it to me* gesture. "Come on then, show me this clue, because I assure you, I am not part of the treasure hunt."

Reaching into the pocket of his shorts, he pulled out a crumpled slip of yellow paper and handed it to me.

If you want to pick up this leaf,
Holding it tightly might be folly.
Because it's easy to get pricked,
When you touch a piece of _ _ _ _ _.

"Holly." I whispered the answer to the riddle, my mind whirling. Glancing at the sweating man in front of me, I asked, "And how do you know my name is Holly?"

He shrugged. "We asked around."

I barely contained the eye roll. I smiled, although it didn't reach my eyes. "Listen up, folks. I know you *think* you solved this riddle because it's true my name *is* Holly, but seriously, I am not the answer. And looking at this clue, may I suggest you look for a *plant* rather than a person?"

There was a collective murmuring and head nodding before they made their way single file out of the garage. Not a single apology for trespassing and invading my privacy to be had. Shaking my head, I returned to the house, yet even in that short expanse of time, more people were knocking on my front door.

Half an hour later, and we had a problem. There had to be at least twenty people in my front garden, trampling the weeds and arguing with me about the darn clue. I was hot, irritated, and ready to zap their butts into next week. I'd texted Doris for backup, and a wave of relief washed over me when her red Impala roared down the street and skidded to a stop out front, narrowly missing a couple who were studying their map, heads close together as they glanced at it, then me, then back to the map.

Elbowing her way through the throng of treasure hunters, she joined me on the warped front porch. "What on earth is going on?"

"They think I'm the answer to their stupid riddle," I grumbled, fed up with the whole thing. "The answer is holly, but it's not me, it's the plant. But none of them believe me and they won't leave."

The crowd started jeering at me, calling me a spoilsport and accusing me of not playing the game in the spirit intended. My temper rose, magic dancing across my knuckles. Clenching my fists, I glared at them, willing them to leave before I did something I'd regret, like turning them all into bunches of holly.

Doris patted my shoulder. "I've got just the thing."

I watched as she pushed her way back through the crowd and popped the trunk of her car, rummaged around, then stood back, holding up a bag triumphantly. It wasn't until she reached inside and began throwing the contents at those closest to her that I realized what the bag contained.

Doris was throwing tomatoes. Possibly rotten tomatoes, for they were definitely splatting and liquifying as they made contact with her targets.

"Go on!" she yelled, winding up for another

direct hit. "Get out of here. Holly isn't part of your silly treasure hunt. Take a hint and go find the real clue!"

Squeals intermingled with the sound of tomatoes exploding against flesh rang out loud enough to wake the dead, but rather than leave, the crowd began scooping up tomato remnants and throwing them at not only Doris, but each other.

Splat! Half a tomato hit my chest with a squelch. Tomato juice and pulp oozed into my cleavage before I dug my fingers in and scooped it out. There was yelling. There was throwing. There were tomatoes everywhere. And then there was the whoop of a police siren and flashing lights. All the while, I remained on the stoop, wondering how this had become my life. Doris hurried to my side, dripping with tomato remnants.

"What's going on here?" Calder demanded, hands on hips as he surveyed the tomato carnage.

No one spoke. I'd like to think they'd suddenly realized they were grown adults who'd lost their good sense, but somehow I doubted it. More likely, they were feeling a little sheepish at getting caught acting so childish but not exactly regretting their actions, for I'd seen their faces when hurling tomatoes at each other. They were having fun.

When no one answered, Calder tried again. "Who's in charge here?"

"I am." Only the voice that answered didn't come from my front garden but farther down the street. We turned to watch as Jensen Chapman approached, ball cap pulled low, backpack strapped on. Sweat darkened his T-shirt, and he wiped the back of a wrist across his brow. He stopped when he reached Doris's car, eyes widening at the sea of red rapidly soaking into the soil of what I loosely termed my garden.

"Oh, geez," he muttered, first eyeing the mess, then the bedraggled crowd responsible. "Guys?"

Now everyone spoke. At once. They surged around Jensen, all keen to explain themselves and what had happened and apparently blame me for not playing the game. While Jensen tried to soothe the pack of treasure hunters, Calder skirted around them and joined us on the porch.

"You okay?" His eyes drifted to my chest and the evidence of the direct hit I'd taken. My cheeks flamed with heat.

"I'm fine. It'll wash out." I eyed the tomato stain, wondering if it would, in fact, wash out.

Calder's eyes moved to Doris. "I can only assume you're responsible for this?"

"Who? Me?" She batted her eyelashes, then grinned. "You betcha. Bunch of morons can't even read a clue properly, and then they have the nerve to accuse Holly of lying! I mean, why would she? Idiots. You should arrest them all, Calder. Disturbing the peace."

He turned to face the crowd, his arm brushing mine as he stood by my side. A frisson of delight danced through my body at the contact.

"Well, I could, Doris, but that would mean arresting you, too. I mean, I'm up for it if you don't mind being squeezed into a cell with this crowd?"

"What?" she squeaked. "That's outrageous! I demand my own cell."

I couldn't contain the giggle that escaped. Trust Doris not to bat an eyelid at being arrested but to take umbrage to the idea of sharing a prison cell. When Calder's fingers curled around mine, my heart practically stopped, only to resume again with an ever-increasing rhythm. Shooting him a look out of the corner of my eye, I left my hand in his. His presence soothed my frayed nerves. And that was something I'd need a little time to sit down and unpack and ponder over.

"So, what's this clue that's got them all riled up?" he asked me, content to stand by my side and hold my hand as we watched Jensen calm the treasure hunters.

I heaved a sigh and repeated the riddle.

"That's barely a riddle," Doris complained. "Even a child could work out the answer is holly."

"Yes," I agreed. "But the riddle is clearly talking about a plant. Not a person."

"That's the thing with riddles," Calder said. "The answers can often be misconstrued."

"I'm so sorry about all of this," Jensen said, making his way up the path. Behind him, the crowd slowly dispersed, heading back into town, complaining about the heat and stickiness of being covered in tomatoes. "I don't know how this happened."

"Not much of a riddle if you ask me." Doris sniffed in disdain, but to my surprise, Jensen nodded in agreement.

"That's just it. That riddle—or clue—is not part of the treasure hunt."

"What?" all three of us said in unison.

Jensen slung his backpack off his shoulders and rummaged inside, eventually pulling out a crumpled piece of paper. Unfolding it, he held it out to Calder, who released my hand to take it. "This is my blueprint. This house definitely isn't on it." While

Calder glanced at the hand-drawn map with notes scrawled over it, Jensen pulled out a dog-eared notebook. "And these are the clues." Flipping open to the relevant page, he handed it to me. "See? No mention of Holly, either the plant or you, in here anywhere."

"So, someone is handing out fake clues? Who?" I was annoyed all over again that someone had targeted me intentionally. But why? I didn't understand what anyone would have to gain by doing such a thing other than to get under my skin.

Jensen stubbed his toes on a weed filled crack and shrugged his shoulders. "That's the thing. Each of them said they got this clue from a different source."

"You're saying you can't pinpoint where this fake clue started?" Calder's voice took on a tone I recognized. Cop mode. I glanced at him, wondering what had piqued his interest. Seconds ago, he hadn't seemed all that concerned.

Jensen nodded. "Here, let me show you." He began pointing at locations on his map. "For example, one clue was picked up at River's café. But then another contestant was at the florist, Back to the Fuchsia, and they picked up the clue there. And yet another was at Sew it Seams, the clothing alteration place that Roselyn Park runs out of her home. See? All different stages of the treasure hunt. It's weird. I don't understand how it happened. Or who did it, because honestly, I swear, I don't know you at all—I'm assuming you're the Holly who has everyone in hysterics?" His last words were aimed at me, and I nodded.

"Holly Day," I introduced myself.

His brows shot up. "Seriously?"

"Don't even," I warned.

He stared at me for a moment, blinked, then cleared his throat. "Gotcha." Blowing out a breath, he turned his focus back to Calder. "All I can do is apologize, Sheriff. I know I promised you the treasure hunt wouldn't negatively impact your town, and it seems I've failed." He glanced over his shoulder at the remnants of tomatoes strewn over the ground. "I can't explain any of it."

"May I suggest you revisit your clue holders and retrieve any remaining fake clues pointing to Holly?" Calder deadpanned.

Jensen recognized a reprieve when he saw it, quickly shoving everything back in his backpack and slinging it over his shoulder as he walked backward down the path, hand raised in salute. "On it. Again, my apologies, Holly."

CHAPTER TEN

"Since you're here," I said to Doris after Calder had left, "I may as well bring you up to speed."

"On?" Doris followed me inside, heading straight for the camp chair placed in front of the AC. Settling in with a wiggle and a strategic fart, which I politely ignored, she angled her face toward the vents, the cool air ruffling her white hair and the scent of tomatoes filling the room.

Heading into the kitchen, I poured us each a coffee, calling to her through the hole in the wall. "Doris, I need to ask you about the powder."

"What about it?"

"It's not striking powder, is it?"

"Nope."

Carrying the coffees into the living room, I

handed her one before taking a seat on the cot, placing my mug on the floor by my feet.

"Why did you say it was?"

Doris eyeballed me, one brow raised.

"What?" I protested.

"You know you have trust issues, right?"

I rolled my neck, trying not to be offended. How could I take offense when she was one hundred percent right? "Yeah," I finally admitted. "So?"

"So, you clearly don't trust Fay—and hey, I'm not saying you have to. You only met her yesterday. But I've known her since the day she was born and while I don't approve of some of her actions—like not coming home for her grandparents' funerals—that doesn't mean she's a bad person."

"But you lied to her."

"A little white lie."

"I still don't get it," I admitted. "Why not say you hadn't worked out what the powder was?"

"Okay, look. I want to try to slow her down a little, cos she's all guns blazing with this investigation, and yeah, sure, she's done some intelligence analysis study but that doesn't mean she's ready for the real thing. I figure if we can keep her close, we can keep an eye on her, make sure she doesn't get herself into any trouble."

"But you were okay with her going on a date with Luke last night? One of our suspects." If that wasn't dangerous, I didn't know what was.

"You don't think I was keeping an eye on her?"

My mouth fell open. "You *spied* on her?"

"Technically, I was spying on Luke. Fay just happened to be there."

I couldn't help it. I burst out laughing. Doris joined in, although I doubted she knew what she was laughing at. Eventually getting myself under control, I wheezed, "And? How did the date go?"

"You know, I was expecting something... hotter. Fay is all sexy siren with her heels and lipstick, but they went to River's—that hardly screams romance —and only stayed half an hour."

"And then what? Back to Fay's hotel?" Even she wouldn't be so foolish as to invite a potential murderer back to her room... would she?

"Nope. They parted ways in front of River's. Not even a kiss goodnight. I'd say that date was a dud."

"Probably for the best if Luke's our killer."

"How about you and Calder?" Doris shot me a sly look. "What happened there? Don't think I didn't notice the little hand holding episode on your front porch."

My face practically glowed neon red. "Yeah, uh," I cleared my throat. "So, he, umm… kissed me."

Doris whooped and fist pumped the air. "'Bout time," she chortled, then sobered, squinting at me. "How did that come about? Dino's murder? He doesn't know you're withholding evidence, does he?"

I shook my head. "I was ill last night. Flynn went and got him, and he showed up and"—I shrugged.—"Basically, he took care of me."

"You were ill?" Doris straightened, her face full of concern. "What happened? Are you okay?"

"It was awful," I confessed. "Calder thinks it was my *allergy*. I had the worst headache, and I was vomiting."

"But you don't have an allergy," she reminded me.

"I know." I shot her a look.

"Oh. So what you're saying is you don't know why you were sick last night?"

"Correct."

"And Calder… what? Stayed the night?"

"Not in the way you're thinking. I was passed out here." I patted the cot I was sitting on. "I think Calder must have spent the night in the camp chair. This morning, he cooked us breakfast."

"How romantic!" Doris swooned.

"It was thoughtful and kind. Not romantic. Although he did do the dishes."

"Holly Day, you need to snap that man up quick smart."

"Doris Shutt, in case you've forgotten, I'm here under false pretenses. I've been lying to him this entire time about who I am, why I'm here. Do you think he'll want a relationship with me when the truth comes out?"

"Oh, honey, is that what's bothering you?" She waved away my concerns. "He'll understand. He likes you for you."

"Yeah, well, if the boot were on the other foot, I'm not sure I'd be so understanding." Doris had said it herself. I had trust issues. And I could hardly expect Calder to trust me when I couldn't bring myself to tell him the truth. It was a no-win situation and any romantic notions best forgotten about. My heart, on the other hand, was in disagreement with my head, insisting a relationship with Calder was a wonderful idea and I should pursue it with gusto.

"We need to get back to Dino's murder," I grumbled, not liking the tug-of-war between heart and head. "So, if the powder isn't striking powder, what is it? And how are we going to identify it now that the sample has been destroyed?"

"Actually, I still have some. It's on the slide under the microscope. But we probably don't need it, anyway. I have my notes."

"And we have John Smith's journal." I retrieved the book from the kitchen. "I was thinking about the rune carved into Dino's hand. It's the same rune Denise used to hex Seth and John."

"Denise can't be responsible for this," Doris pointed out. "She's locked up."

"But maybe she wasn't acting alone. Remember how she was babbling about becoming a member of the Shadow Binder Covenant, binding herself to the underworld and creating a conduit for a Draughr to cross dimensions?"

"That was the ramblings of a crazy woman." Doris waved it away as nonsense.

"But what if it wasn't? We've found out a lot since then. Like John Smith's journal, for example. Maybe that talks about the Shadow Binder Covenant? There could be others. Maybe they're behind Dino's death?"

"Does it? Did you find something?"

"Nah, not yet. Got interrupted." Resuming my seat on the cot, I opened the journal on my lap. Doris made a move to join me, but I shook my head.

"Nope. You're not getting tomato juice all over my bed. Drag the chair over or stay where you are."

"You're skating on thin eggshells, Holly Day," Doris grumbled, but she dragged the chair across to the cot, and I scooched up to the end so she could read over my shoulder.

My eyes scanned as I flicked through the pages, not stopping until a word leaped out at me. Actually, it was two words. "Shadowfall Amulet," I read out loud.

"What's that?" Doris asked.

"No idea, but I think Denise said something about a Shadowfall Amulet. Didn't she?" The words were so familiar to me, like I'd heard them before. *Shadowfall Amulet...*

"That woman was almost talking in tongues," Doris huffed. "We can't believe a word of it."

"Maybe, maybe not, but it can't be a coincidence that Dino Cittadino turns up dead with that exact same rune carved into his palm. Right? It has to be connected. Listen to this, it says you need the Shadowfall Amulet and the Codex of the Solstice to open the Obsidian Field." My breath caught when I turned the page. "Holy guacamole!"

"What?" Doris leaned in closer. "What's that?"

"It's a sketch of the Codex." I held the book up so she could see.

"Looks just like the soul stone, doesn't it?"

I swiveled to look at her. "Doris! It *is* the soul stone. Or should I say, what we thought was a soul stone is actually the Codex of the Solstice? We have to get it out of the tree. Now." Flinging the book onto the cot next to me, I hauled myself upright, waiting for Doris to join me. She was taking her sweet time about it.

"What's the sudden rush?" she grumbled. "It's perfectly fine in the tree."

"You don't think it's a coincidence that all these treasure hunters were targeting me? That a false clue led them here, to my house? They're after the stone." Panic rippled over me, sending electric shocks down my nerve endings, making me twitchy and itchy and giving me this relentless sense of urgency.

Doris clamped a hand on my shoulder. "Calm down, love. You're starting to sound like Denise, a little bit crazy pants."

"Doris!" I wailed, a sense of dread I couldn't shake washing over me. Maybe that's why I'd found the house so oppressive lately, because it was at the crux of something bad about to happen. If the soul stone was the Codex of the Solstice, then whoever was behind this only needed the Shadowfall Amulet and they'd have everything they needed to open another dimension. And whether or not you believed it possible, it was a bad idea. Dimensions were not meant to be crossed.

"Relax, no one knows you have it," Doris said, following me to the back door.

"That's just it. I think they do. I think they've just left it here until they need it, and then they'll collect it when they're ready."

Doris stopped, and I turned, impatience making my magic prickle and dance over my skin. Flynn, who'd been dozing God only knows where, suddenly appeared, running up my body to my shoulder, prepared to lick me to distract me from using my magic.

"Don't," I growled, pulling my power back, coiling it around me. "I'm not going to use it." One of the rules when Harding had hidden me in Gravestone was *do not use your magic*. Despite Gravestone having the ability to hide magic, there was the possibility that I could still be traced. Better safe than sorry.

"You know." Doris pushed past me, flinging open the back door and standing on the rickety stoop. "You may have a point. Not about the treasure

hunters. They're a bunch of humans with no clue."
She shot me a cheesy grin at her pun, which I weakly
returned. "But let's say all of this *is* connected. If
there is such a thing as the Shadow Binder
Covenant, like Denise claimed, then it only makes
sense that there's more than one member. Big magic
needs big power, drawing—most likely—from a big
coven."

"Others are coming." My eyes shot to the massive
cedar elm tree towering over my back yard. At the
top, taped to the branches, was the soul stone. Flynn
began squeaking in my ear. It sounded like a lecture,
but I couldn't be sure because I didn't speak rat.

"Flynn has a point," Doris said, turning to go
back inside.

"What? You speak rat now?" I asked, following
her.

"I'm pretty sure he's asking what you intend to
do with the soul stone—or the Codex of the
Saltshaker—once you get it out of the tree. Is there a
safer place?"

I staggered to a stop. If that was what Flynn was
saying, then he was right, darn it. We'd hidden it in
the tree because that was the safest place we could
think of. And logic told me to leave it where it was.
But this sense of urgency and panic would not leave.

I was as on edge as a squirrel in the fall with zero nut collection.

"Doris, let's go to your house."

"Sure. I need to get cleaned up, anyway."

I grabbed my laptop and John Smith's journal, shoving them both into my backpack before following Doris out to her Impala. The tomato juice from the earlier food fight had dried, staining the dirt a deep, dark red, not unlike dried blood.

"Oh, pretty." Doris practically skipped down the garden path while I limped along behind, the sense of dread clinging to me like a second skin.

CHAPTER ELEVEN

"Damn right I'm pretty."

"I said petty."

"Tomato, potato." Doris fluffed her stark white hair, the curls teased to within an inch of their life and sprayed with enough hair spray to hold her life together. If she cared for such things, which she didn't.

"You can't tell me this little vendetta with our esteemed mayor is worth all this trouble?" Kerris Jones was not a nice woman. Nevertheless, she held a position of power, and it didn't pay to deliberately antagonize her. She had connections and wasn't above using them to get her own way or make your life miserable, preferably both. Which she did. Frequently.

Doris had been determined to catch Dino and Kerris in *flagrante delicto* ever since Dino had used Kerris as an alibi in the murder of Cody Pendant. Whether the two of them were really sleeping together was another matter. Cody's killer had been caught—it wasn't Dino—so we never got to the bottom of his alibi. Bogus or not, he'd still broken into my house, and now that he, too, had been murdered, Doris was more determined than ever to find out if Mayor Kerris Jones was involved.

"Do you really think Kerris is a member of the Shadow Binder Covenant?" I almost wished we hadn't stumbled upon that little nugget of information, for Doris had clearly been pondering it while taking a shower. Once she'd washed the tomato stain from her skin, she'd come out with a new—*fierce*—determination to expose the mayor as a murderer.

"We have the proof she's up to something. She called Dino the night he was killed."

"Yes, she did, but it was a phone call. We don't have a transcript. They could have been discussing anything."

Doris reached over and grabbed my arm, fingers digging in painfully. "Look!" she hissed. "Who's that she's meeting?"

"Ease up." I pried her fingers off my arm and followed her gaze out the front windshield of her bright red Impala. Despite Doris being retired SIA, she'd yet to learn that her easily recognizable car did not make a sensible stake out choice.

"Whoa," I whispered, watching . Luke Bizzy currently in an intense discussion with Kerris. Doris let out a wolf whistle.

"He's hot, I'll give him that," she said.

"He sure gets around." The man was not only handsome, but he had that dangerous edge to him that women found irresistible. A date with Fay last night, now a little tête-à-tête with Kerris. Even as I watched, I couldn't shake the feeling that Luke and I had met before, yet even as I wracked my brain for those lost memories, I still came up empty.

Doris leaned into the back seat for her purse and pulled out a pair of binoculars, unashamedly focusing on the pair. "Well, I can tell you this isn't a romantic liaison," Doris said. "Kerris is positively fuming. Unless it is a romantic liaison and he turned her down," she speculated.

"Yeah, looking at Luke Bizzy, I hardly think the mayor is his type. Fay, on the other hand... you were at their date last night. What did you think?"

"How do you mean?"

"Fay said Luke is here representing a charity—that he's a freelancer PR person. And Fay's here as a social media influencer, to pimp the treasure hunt. Were they really on a date? Or was it a business meeting?"

"You think she lied to us about it being a date?"

"I think she has an image to uphold."

A whirring and clicking sound alerted me to the fact that Doris had replaced the binoculars with a blow your mind massive camera, with a lens so huge the paparazzi would be jealous, and was now taking photos of Luke and Kerris. Subtle was not her strong suit.

I'm not sure what alerted Kerris to our presence. Was it the flash of sun on the camera lens or Doris leaning out the window and yelling, "Yoo-hoo! Kerris! How about a money shot?"

Either way, she saw us and was now pounding sand in our direction, a thunderous glower on her face.

"Time to go, hotshot." Grabbing the camera from her, I sat it on my lap while Doris gunned the engine and shot off down the street with enough Gs to have my neck snapping back. Driving with Doris had me in a constant state of whiplash.

Gripping the dash while we careened around corners, I cast a glance behind us. "It's okay. She's not following."

Doris eased her foot off the accelerator a fraction. "What do you think that was all about?"

"Kerris and Luke? No idea, but it looked intense. And we know Luke was in contact with Dino. Could well be the reason Dino sponsored the treasure hunt, as a cover for why he was really here—to purchase something, an occult object I assume, from Luke."

"Only Luke changed the terms of their deal. Jacked up the price," Doris said.

"Now a person usually only does that when they discover the item they're selling is more valuable than they realized."

"Or when they have you over a barrel," Doris added. "Like, they know you *really* want something. Like... really, really want it."

"And are prepared to pay anything to get it."

"You're thinking it's the Shadowfall Amulet? The last piece needed to open this Obsidian Field thing?"

"I mean, it's a possibility." I chewed my lip, mulling it over.

"We should tell Calder what we know," Doris said, surprising me.

"What? Why?"

"Because he can help us."

"You think he's going to help us? He made a point of telling me to keep my nose out of this investigation."

Doris snorted. "You don't think he actually believed you would, do you? He was only saying that because he had to. As sheriff. You know, a duty of care type thing."

"Like the *don't leave town* comment?"

"When did he say that?"

"At the rotunda."

She shot me a look, her eyes twinkling.

"What? What's that look for?"

"You can take one man's trash to another man's treasure, but you can't make it drink."

I burst out laughing. "Doris, what does that even mean?"

"It means I think it's high time you and the sheriff sat down and had a proper conversation."

"We talk," I protested.

"Holly Day, do not think for one minute that I don't know you tie yourself up in knots over that man, that it bothers you more than you care to admit that you're lying to him on a daily basis. And you wanna know the simplest solution to that?

Stop lying. Just tell him the truth. Heck, he knows he can trust you. You saw him in bear form and haven't told a soul. If that ain't love, I don't know what is."

"Love?" I choked, my spit going down the wrong way and making me cough and my eyes water. "We're not talking about love. Lust maybe."

"Fine, whatever, ignore me." Doris huffed. "If you can't tell him the truth about yourself, then at least give him a carrot about the case."

"A carrot?" Doris was speaking in riddles. She had my head spinning.

She sighed and rolled her eyes. "Take Dino's phone to Calder, Holly. Think of it as a peace offering."

"He's going to be mad I stole it."

"Probably."

Pulling into her driveway, she kept the engine idling. "Well?" she prompted.

"Oh! You mean *now?*"

"No time like the present! You go grab the phone, and I'll drop you off at the station."

She didn't drop me at the station. We were on our way when we spotted Luke and Kerris. Again! Only Luke was leaving on foot, and Kerris was getting in her car.

"Quick, get out!" Doris jerked the car to a stop. "You follow him, I'll tail Kerris."

Opening the door, I practically fell out of the car. "Try to be discrete this time, huh?" But my words fell on deaf ears as Doris roared away in hot pursuit of the mayor.

Darting behind one of the massive trees lining each side of the road, I pressed myself to the trunk, then cautiously peered around it. Luke was strolling casually along the sidewalk, hands in pockets, seemingly without a care in the world. I followed, hobbling as quietly as I could with the thunking noise the walking boot made, constantly darting behind trees in case he suddenly turned around and discovered me stalking him.

I followed him down Main Street, onto the Esplanade, and then to Porter Road.

"He's heading to the police station."

I must have said it out loud, for he paused, looking back over his shoulder, while I plastered myself to yet another tree trunk. My clothes clung to me with sweat, and the bark from the tree added another layer of discomfort, irritating my already irritated skin. How did Luke look so cool while I was a red, hot, sweaty mess?

By the time he reached the station, I'd fallen

behind. My foot ached, I was hot, and something on the bark of the trees was reacting with my skin in an itchy rash kind of way. This was not how I wanted to appear when confessing to Calder that I'd stolen evidence from a crime scene.

As soon as Luke entered the building, I stepped out onto the footpath, hoping to gain some speed now that I wasn't darting from one tree to another. Smoothing my palms over my shorts, I hurried up the path to the front door, wondering what business Luke had here. Maybe he was turning himself in? Doubtful. He didn't walk like a condemned man. His walk had been relaxed and casual. Maybe Calder already had Dino's phone records—which could be a good thing because he may not be so mad I'd swiped Dino's phone—and had asked Luke to come in to discuss the communication he'd had with Dino.

That seemed the more likely scenario, so I cautiously made my way inside, trying to keep as quiet as possible so I could eavesdrop. The front counter was unattended, and I figured Deputy Biden must still be door knocking. Or on patrol. Either way, it worked in my favor as I skirted around the counter.

Calder's office was down a corridor, the first door on the right. Opposite was a supply closet. I knew this because I'd been marched through the station on more than one occasion on my way to the cells. And this girl paid attention, memorizing the layout, and today was pay off day. Keeping my back to the wall, I crept along until I came to Calder's door. It was partly ajar, giving me enough cover to slip into the closet opposite without being seen, and standing in the closet amongst the shelves of paper, envelopes, and printer toner, I unabashedly listened to the conversation across the hall.

"I've got it under control," Calder was saying. "You don't need to check in."

"Call it professional courtesy. Her and that old broad who drives the red Impala were following me earlier."

I heard a sigh, assumed it was Calder. He was probably running a hand around the back of his neck like he had the habit of doing whenever news of Doris's shenanigans reached his ears. "That'd be Doris Shutt. She's harmless."

"Doris Shutt, huh? Good to know." There was the creaking of a chair, then Luke said, "I've been working this case almost two years and am this close to busting it wide open. Harding couldn't have made it any clearer. Your assignment was simple. Keep an eye on her, keep her safe."

My eyes widened at the mention of my boss, Scott Harding. How did Luke know him? And who was Calder instructed to keep safe? Me? But Calder had lowered his voice, and I couldn't make out what they were saying anymore.

Pondering over the strange conversation I'd heard, I snuck out of the closet and made my way back to the front counter—it wouldn't help my cause if I was discovered eavesdropping outside the sheriff's office. I'd just slammed my palm on the bell to announce my presence when I heard footsteps approaching and Luke Bizzy appeared. His brown eyes swept over me in a familiar way, a slight smile curling his lips. He touched his fingers to the brim of his hat in greeting. "Tess." He nodded once as he skirted the counter and strode past, leaving me with my mouth hanging open.

"Wait," I called after him. "How do you know me?"

But Luke Bizzy didn't pause or look back, his long legs eating up the distance between the police station and the road, already out of earshot.

"Holly?"

Calder's voice behind me made me jump, and I spun, grabbing the counter for balance.

"You okay?" he asked.

Narrowing my eyes, I glared at him. "*What* is going on here?" There was no doubt in my mind that Sheriff Joshua Calder and Luke Bizzy were in cahoots. And Luke had just called me by my real name, Tess. There was definitely more to this situation than met the eye, and Calder was about to tell me what it was. I'd make sure of it.

Calder stiffened, then blinked. "Well, Holly, this is a police station, and right now, I'm investigating a murder." It was the condescending tone that got me. Why, all of a sudden, was he talking to me like I was mentally impaired? I ignored the little voice in my head telling me I was, that my brain had been scrambled and half my memories erased. The surge of rage that roared through me took us both by surprise. Standing on tiptoe, I leaned over the counter, bringing my face close to his. "Tell me what you know," I demanded.

He arched a brow, unconcerned that I was all up in his business. "About?"

I couldn't maintain my balance and had to lower myself back to the floor, losing what had felt like an advantage, although judging by the way Calder's lips twitched, it wasn't the intimidating move I'd thought it was.

"Luke Bizzy. Who is he? And how does he know

who I really am?" As soon as the words left my mouth, I knew I'd messed up.

"Who you really are?" Calder looked confused, then concerned. He stepped around the counter, reaching for my hand. "Come on, you'd better have a seat. I'll get you some water. You look a little... overheated." Which was code for a red hot mess.

Allowing myself to be led back to his office, I chewed my lip and tried to push back the panic sweeping through me. I didn't understand what was going on. My emotions were rocketing from anger to fear with barely a pause in between, and I could feel my magic churning in response to my inner turmoil. The oppressive feeling was back, and I didn't have Flynn to calm me down.

"This was a mistake," I whispered, biting a nail as I sat in Calder's office, waiting for him to return with a glass of water. "I shouldn't be here."

"Why's that?"

I jumped, startled. Placing the water on the desk in front of me, Calder took his seat on the opposite side and watched me. My hand shook as I reached for the water. My gaze ricocheted around the room, touching on every little detail yet absorbing none of it. My burning need for the truth was causing an existential crisis, I was sure of it.

I'd come to the police station to turn over Dino's phone, I reminded myself. Stick to the plan, that's all I needed to do. Doris thought I should tell Calder the truth, and I'd been working my way up to it until I'd overheard his conversation with Luke, and then Luke had called me by my real name, and now I wasn't sure what to make of any of it. I was also reasonably confident that my brain was melting.

"Holly?" Calder prompted.

Chewing my lip, I sucked in a breath and blurted, "I'm an SIA agent." It was like ripping off a Band-aid. Better done fast.

"I know," Calder said, unperturbed.

I stared at him in disbelief, my mind whirling. "What? How do you know? When?"

"I've known ever since you arrived."

I sat there with my mouth hanging open in shock. I'd spent all this time agonizing over whether I could trust him with this and he'd known all along? Then anger crept in, anger that he'd known and hadn't said anything, let me keep on thinking I was maintaining my cover. Snapping my mouth closed, I shoved my chair back, rising to my feet.

"You *knew?*" Blood pounded in my ears, and I struggled to hold on to my composure. I felt like a fool.

His hazel eyes swept over me, taking in my stance, my rigid shoulders and clenched jaw. "Hey," he soothed. "It's okay. Harding reached out. Asked me to keep an eye out for you."

"Harding *told* you?" I been battling to keep my identity a secret, and to learn it had been a fruitless exercise from the start had me seeing red. Calder stood, reaching for me, but I backed away.

"Don't touch me." I felt betrayed. By Harding and by Calder. Oh, how they must have laughed about me behind my back. Poor, foolish agent Tess Hunter, memory riddled with holes, needs someone to keep an eye on her in Gravestone because she's more of a hinderance than an asset.

"Holly, please sit down. Let's talk about this."

Sucking in a deep breath, I tipped my head back and looked at the ceiling, trying to center myself, trying to calm my thundering heart and wayward emotions. After a minute, I closed my eyes, blew out the breath I'd been holding and gave up trying to make sense out of any of this.

"Is Luke Bizzy SIA?" I asked, voice eerily calm.

"Yes."

Which explained how he knew me and why he seemed so familiar. We'd probably worked together at some point. Snapping my eyes open, I reached into my back pocket and pulled out Dino's phone.

"Here." I handed it to Calder. "This is Dino's." Spinning on my heel, I stalked out of the police station, ignoring his calls for me to return. The truth was out—he'd known all along—and there would be no going back.

CHAPTER TWELVE

Calder blew up my phone, and I took morbid delight in rejecting each and every call. Of course, he could lock up the station and follow me, but I suspected he wouldn't. He had a town full of treasure hunters to deal with. Closing the police station wasn't an option. Instead, he'd have to call Deputy Biden back and wait for her to take over before he could leave, which suited me just fine. I needed time and space.

Pushing through the door of Rivers café, I headed toward the table I usually shared with Doris and took a seat. I'd barely picked up the menu when the bell above the door chimed, and I glanced up to see Doris charging inside.

"There you are!" she declared, taking the seat opposite. "What are we having?"

I tossed the menu on the table. "Anything. You choose. I don't care."

"Oh dear. Was Calder mad about the phone?" Doris sympathized.

"He knew," I hissed, leaning across the table. "He's known all along that I'm SIA. Harding *called* him."

"Oh." She nodded, then said, "Ooooooh."

"Exactly." I sat back, folding my arms across my chest.

"But that's a good thing, isn't it? Because he knows. And now you know he knows. So, no more lies, yeah? Which was what you wanted."

"I guess." She was right. Let's face it, Doris had a habit of being right. But it still stung, and I had to laugh at myself because this would be exactly how Calder would feel right now if he hadn't known and I'd just told him. Only the shoe was on the other foot, and it was me left smarting. "This was not how I expected it to go down."

"Twice in one day, ladies." River approached, her smile wide.

"How goes the treasure hunt?" Doris asked. The café was empty except for us, not a hunter in sight. It was blissful.

"All good, although I hear you had some excitement, Holly. Someone planted a fake clue, so people harassed you?"

"You heard about that, huh?"

"Jensen was in earlier, going through the pile of clues he left me to hand out to make sure there weren't any of the fake ones amongst them." River patted my shoulder. "Sorry that happened to you. I know you value your privacy."

"What was your clue? For this place?" Doris asked.

"Oh, um, let me see if I remember it." River squished up her face while trying to remember.

> *"What can run but never walks,*
> *Has a mouth but never talks,*
> *Has a head but never weeps,*
> *Has a bed but never sleeps?"*

"A river. Clever. So, people either came to the café or they came to you, the person," I said.

River nodded. "Yep. One and the same, really. Can I interest you ladies in the special? Apple pie with ice cream and a milkshake?"

"You know what"—I smiled—"that sounds perfect."

"Make it two," Doris declared, tossing her menu onto the table.

"Coming right up." River hurried away to get our order while I sat and pondered the treasure hunt, grateful to have something to focus on other than Calder and, you know, the truth.

I sighed.

"What was that for?" Doris asked.

"What?"

"The sigh."

I waved my hand in dismissal. "Nothing. It doesn't matter. How did it go with Kerris?"

Doris snorted. "Snoretown. She went back to work. We need to find out why she was meeting with Luke Bizzy."

"Oh yeah. About Luke. He's SIA, so he's not our killer."

"He's what now?"

"Yup. Followed him to the police station. Overheard him talking with Calder. He's an agent. And he called me by my real name, so he knows who I am."

Doris blinked. "Oh. Well. Anyway, that doesn't mean that he isn't the killer. He could have gone rogue!"

I chuckled softly, fiddling with a napkin. "I somehow doubt that, but sure, okay."

"You're probably right." It was Doris's turn to sigh. "He's probably not our killer. But guess who's been central in almost all of this?"

"Who?"

"Kerris." Doris began counting off on her fingers. "She had some sort of relationship with Dino, whether it was personal, professional, or both. We saw her in here being rude to Fay. Then we saw her in a heated argument with Luke. She's had a busy day with arguments. Maybe she had one with Dino."

"Her confrontation with Fay was odd but not out of character. Obviously, she'd heard Fay was back in town and took it upon herself to poke her nose in Fay's business. Only Fay knew exactly what buttons to push to get a reaction," I said. "And the stuff with Luke? Well, now that we know he's SIA, he was probably asking questions she didn't want to answer —like what, exactly, was Dino Cittadino to her."

"That's what we need to find out," Doris said.

"What we need to find out is, did Kerris have the opportunity to kill Dino? And if so, what was her motive? Why now?"

"We're missing one glaring thing," Doris said.

"What's that?"

"This was a ritualistic killing, and Kerris isn't a witch."

"That we know of," I pointed out. "She could still be a member of the Shadow Binder Covenant."

"How do we find that out?"

"I wish I knew."

The bell above the door tinkled, followed by the sound of heels click clacking across the floor. "There you are!" Fay greeted us with smiles and air kisses, pulling up a third chair to our table for two. "I was looking for you."

"You found us," I quipped.

"So." She leaned her elbows on the table. "How goes the investigation?"

"Where have you been?" Doris cut in before I had a chance to even consider how to answer Fay's question.

Fay waved a hand. "After the *official* opening of the treasure hunt by *moi,* I took a few selfies around town to post to the socials. Gotta get those hashtags trending." Pulling out her phone, she showed Doris the photos she'd taken, and the two of them went on a ten-minute instructional on how to take the perfect selfie.

Just as our order arrived, the bell above the door

chimed again, and I glanced over Doris's shoulder to see Jensen Chapman slip inside. I figured he was here for treasure hunt business, but when he took a seat and picked up the menu, I decided I was wrong.

"Hey, Jensen." River gave him a smile as she weaved her way to our table with our order. "I'll be with you in a second. Oh! Hi, Fay, I didn't hear you come in. Can I get you something, hun?"

"Well, that apple pie sure looks good. I'll have what they're having, please."

"Sure thing. Milkshake too?"

"Absolutely."

I half listened to Fay and Doris chatting away while I stuffed my face with apple pie and watched Jensen Chapman, who, in turn, was taking clandestine photos of River.

When River returned with Fay's order, I asked her, "Do you know Jensen?" I jerked my head toward the man sitting on his own.

"Only as an acquaintance," River said with a shrug.

"So, you didn't know him before this?" *This* being the treasure hunt.

"Nope. Why?"

"Just wondering." I shrugged. I needed to find out why Jensen was taking photos of River before I threw him under the bus. Because once River found out, she'd most likely belt him around the head with one of her pans.

I'd turned my attention back to my pie when I caught Fay watching me.

"What?" I snapped.

Fay raised a brow but waited until River had walked away before saying, "Why the interest in Jensen?"

"You must know him." I avoided answering. "What with him inviting you to open the treasure hunt and all."

"I know him a little, but we're not best friends or anything, if that's what you're asking. I repeat, why the sudden interest in Jensen?"

"Yeah, Holly," Doris chimed in. "What's up?"

"He's taking photos of River. I want to know why."

"What?" Doris and Fay chimed simultaneously while spinning in their seats to gawk at Jensen, who hurriedly put his phone down and picked up his menu.

"Leave it to me." Fay started to stand, but I grabbed her wrist, stopping her.

"No. Sit," I demanded. She sat, blinking her false eyelashes and assuming a hurt expression.

"I'm only trying to help," she protested.

"This requires a little tact and finesse." I shot a look at Doris. "Which is why *I* will talk to Jensen."

Fay looked like she was going to argue, but Doris patted her hand. "Leave it with Holly, love. She's had a bad day. Best to not get in her way."

"Yes, but she's hardly queen of tact and finesse now, is she?" Fay hissed. "I would be the better choice in this scenario. Plus, I know Jensen better than she does."

Ignoring them both, I stood and made my way across the café, sliding into the empty seat opposite Jensen. He'd seen me coming, so by the time I sat down, he had a resigned look on his face.

"Hi." My lips stretched across my teeth in a semblance of a smile.

"You saw." Jensen lowered his head, finding a sudden interest in his navel.

"You taking photos of River? Yes, I did." Placing my hand palm up on the table, I asked, "May I?"

Jensen picked up his phone, unlocked it, and placed it in my palm. I had to school my face to hide my shock. I seriously hadn't thought he'd comply. I'd thought he'd tell me to get lost and mind my own business. Instead, he was acting like a naughty boy who'd just been busted stealing cookies by his mom.

I swiped through his photos. He'd taken at least a dozen of River while we'd been eating our apple pie. Then there were at least a hundred of treasure hunters around town, some of them good, some of them blurry. A photographer, he was not. I was scrolling like I was spinning the wheel on a slot machine when something caught my eye and I had to scroll back to find the photo that had whizzed past.

"This is River with Seth." I held the phone up so I could show him the smiling couple.

He shrugged. "Yeah."

"So, you know River?" I was confused. Why had River lied about knowing Jensen?

But Jensen shook his head. "No. I knew Seth. Well, I knew Seth a little bit."

"Enough to take this photo of the two of them."

He chewed his lip and studied his navel once more. I waited for him to spit out the truth. Eventually, he did. "I got Seth to AirDrop it to me. Told him it was a great photo, and I wanted to get it framed for them, as a surprise."

"And did you?" I already knew he didn't.

"They broke up!"

"Is that why you chose Gravestone for the

treasure hunt? So you could continue to stalk River?"

His head snapped back as if I'd slapped him. "No! No way. I'm not a stalker." I snorted, watching a tide of red sweep across his cheeks. "Okay, fine. I know *this* doesn't look good, but I'm not stalking her, I swear. When the mayor reached out to me, suggesting Gravestone could benefit from one of my treasure hunts, I admit it didn't take much to convince me."

"Because you knew River lives here."

"Because I knew River lives here. And I hadn't seen her in months. Not since her and Seth broke up."

"You know he's dead, right?"

Jensen's jaw dropped. "What?" he squeaked. "When? How?"

"I can't speak for the how, but the when was not long after he got caught not only cheating on River but swindling the townsfolk out of their hard-earned dollars. Everyone thought he'd done a runner. Turns out he was dead."

Jensen audibly gulped. "I did not know that."

"So you weren't friends. Not really."

He shook his head. "Not really."

"Did you know about the girl Seth was seeing in

Corpus Christi?" It seemed to me if Jensen had been aware of that information, he'd have found a way to get it to River. It would benefit him for her to be single.

Jensen shook his head. "If I'd known…" He trailed off, not finishing the sentence.

"You would have told her?"

"I would have *wanted* to." Jensen's puppy dog eyes landed on River, busy behind the counter. "I could never bring myself to approach her. Ask her out."

Which was all kinds of sad. A grown man too nervous to approach the woman he had a crush on and ask her out on a date. This was why I didn't do relationships. So messy.

"Until the treasure hunt gave you the perfect excuse to talk to her. Tell me about our mayor, Kerris Jones. What did she say? Exactly?"

He was still watching River, distracted. "Oh, something about how she'd heard I organized treasure hunts and how she'd like me to do one for Gravestone."

"So, it was her idea?"

"Yeah."

"And did she decide the date?"

"Yeah, she did. Why?"

It was my turn to shrug. "No reason. Just curious.

The mayor made it sound like this whole treasure hunt thing was your idea."

"She did? Oh, well, if that's what she wants to tell people, I don't care either way."

But I did. Everywhere I turned, Kerris was involved. She'd invited Jensen to town. She'd orchestrated the whole treasure hunt. Why? To lure Dino back to Gravestone?

"What do you know about Dino Cittadino?"

"The guy who was killed? Nothing."

"You didn't have any dealings with him?"

"Well, yeah, of course. He was a sponsor of the treasure hunt."

"And how did that come about?"

Jensen tipped his head and looked up at the ceiling, casting his mind back. "You know... I think it may have been the mayor who put us in touch?" He shot me a panicked look. "Listen, I don't want to get her in trouble or anything, okay? She's the mayor and she can be... formidable."

"You mean terrifying." I smirked.

"I just don't want any trouble."

"Do you think there's the slightest chance our esteemed mayor had the opportunity to slip some fake clues into the mix?" I suggested sweetly. Jensen's eyes practically bugged out of his head.

"You think she's the person behind that?" He leaned toward me, the most animated I'd seen him since we started talking.

I shrugged. "Dunno. Did she have the opportunity?"

Jensen looked toward the front window as he considered. "Let me think." He chewed a nail while I sat and waited. Even if Kerris was behind the fake clues, I still couldn't prove it.

"She said she'd call a special council meeting or something to give me the opportunity to deliver the clues around town without people suspecting."

"Is that what usually happens?"

He shook his head. "Nah. I have a team of volunteers who help and we divide up the clues, so even if you saw one of us, you wouldn't know where all the clues were."

"But no team this time?"

"The mayor suggested, since Gravestone is so small, that I could manage the event by myself."

"Interesting. Go on, so you met with the mayor when you arrived?"

He nodded. "Yeah, just a courtesy, really. Everything was in place. She'd given me a list of suggestions for the clues—your name was not among them, by the way—I changed some of them, which seemed to annoy her. She asked to see the clues, but I declined. That annoyed her, too. But I explained I didn't want her compromised and that it was better if she didn't know. That way, she wouldn't reveal anything unintentionally."

"And the media presence? Luke Bizzy, who I understand is liaison for the charity you're fundraising for? And Fay Tality? The social media influencer who opened the treasure hunt. Is that normal?"

"Yeah, sometimes. Not usually for a town of this size, though. To have an influencer open, it is unusual. Usually it would be the mayor or some other official person."

I glanced over at Fay and Doris, who had their heads close together, almost the same shade of platinum blonde. Only Doris's was natural and I suspected Fay's was out of a bottle.

"And was it the mayor who suggested Fay?"

Jensen shook his head. "Fay reached out to me herself when she heard I was conducting a hunt in Gravestone. Said it was her hometown and it would be a hoot to come back and show the backwater bas—" He cut himself off and cleared his throat. "Um, to show the townsfolk how well she's done for herself, or words to that effect."

Sliding Jensen's phone back across the table, I said, "May I suggest you delete those and just talk to her? Stalking is not an acceptable way to get a woman's attention."

"But what do I say?"

"You say hi, can I buy you a coffee? And if she says no, you respect that answer. Understood?" He nodded, and I rose to my feet. "Oh, and Jensen, if I hear you've been creeping on River—or anyone for that matter—I will remove your intestines via your nostrils. Understood?" I added just enough menace to my tone to let him know I wasn't kidding. His head mimicked a bobblehead and his face paled.

"I won't. I promise," he squeaked, then his gaze shifted from me over my shoulder, and I could hear River approaching. I left them to it, returning to Doris and Fay.

"You had quite the discussion," Doris said. "Do tell."

"Kerris Jones is in this up to her neck," I said.

CHAPTER THIRTEEN

"I'm not breaking into Kerris's house again." The last time, I'd almost been a snack for her dog, Jasper. Plus, I hadn't found anything incriminating... except for the blueprints for the proposed boardwalk through the mangroves, which reminded me I'd snapped a photo of the plans and hadn't taken the time to study them. It was time I found out what, exactly, Kerris had planned for the mangroves and my house.

"Fine, I'll do it," Doris said, and I rolled my eyes.

"No, you're not." I turned to include Fay in my glare. "*No one* is breaking into the mayor's house." As both women opened their mouths to argue, I held up my hand to silence them. "Kerris would keep nothing incriminating at her house. If she's involved with the Shadow Binder Covenant, then, like Denise, she'd keep her altar or supplies somewhere else."

"You can't be sure of that," Fay protested. "And what's the Shadow Binder Covenant?"

Darn. I hadn't meant to reveal that little gem to Fay, but it had slipped out. Before I could stop her, Doris told Fay everything except the fact that the soul stone, aka the Codex of the Solstice, was hidden in the elm tree in my back yard.

"Okay, listen." After digesting what Doris had revealed, Fay beckoned us in closer. "I've got this. We don't need to break into Kerris's house. I can find out what we need to know."

"How?" I asked suspiciously.

"Hello?" Fay drawled. "I'm an influencer. You don't think I can turn on the charm to get what I want? Hun, I've been doing this for years. Couple that with my recent training and boom, I'm your woman."

"So, your plan is to simply talk to Kerris and ask her… what? Is she a member of a coven that's trying to open the door to another dimension?" I mean, it would be nice if it were that easy.

"Well, neither of you can do it," she pointed out.

"Yes, but you were seen publicly arguing with her," Doris said.

"Oh pft. That was nothing. I'm not above doing a little schmoozing. Lay on a thick apology, tell her I'd like some photos with her for social media. A little reminiscing about Gravestone, praise her job as mayor. I'll have her eating out of my hand in five minutes flat."

Cocking my head, I studied the younger woman. She had a point. Fay was one of those women men wanted and women wanted to be like. She had this charm and chic style that was inherently appealing, and I got the sense if she wanted something from you, she'd find a way to get it.

"Okay." I shrugged, flopping back in my seat. "Go for it."

"Really?" Her expression was so hopeful that I figured she'd expected me to say no.

"Sure." I stood, digging in my backpack to pay for our apple pie and milkshakes, but Fay beat me to it.

"No, let me." Her smile was wide as she tossed a handful of bills on the table, then linked her elbow with Doris and led the way out of the café. Jensen Chapman watched us leave.

Outside, Fay said, "I'm going to see Kerris now. Might as well strike while the iron is hot. What are you going to do?"

"The library," I blurted. "We're going to the library."

Fay arched a brow but didn't comment other than to say, "I'll call you when I'm done with the mayor."

We watched Fay climb into her red sports car and roar away, only to pull up a short distance later in front of the council chambers.

"It's the heels," Doris answered my silent question. "Our sidewalks are hell to navigate in stilettoes."

"I won't ask how you know that."

"Come on, the library won't wait forever." Doris headed toward the Impala while I followed behind. "Why are we going to the library?"

"Research."

"Urgh. Boring," Doris grumbled, firing up the engine, barely giving me time to slide into the passenger seat before peeling away.

"I was thinking about the Covenant and the Codex of the Solstice and the Shadowfall Amulet. There has to be something about them in the history books, right? Something that connects them to Gravestone, otherwise why is it all happening here?"

"I'm not sure I'm following."

"We know Gravestone was founded on a ley line,

that it can hide mystical energy, right? It got me thinking—why did Denise think she could open the Obsidian Field? It was just her and her tiny altar in Reginald York's house. She didn't have a coven behind her. Rather, she was hexing people to death in her quest to join the Shadow Binder Covenant, of which, as far as we know, there are no other members in town."

"You think the answers are in the history books? That something happened in Gravestone that started all of this." Doris pulled up outside the library and killed the engine.

"I think it can't hurt to look." Overhead, thunder rumbled. Another storm was rolling in.

I followed Doris out of the car, trailing behind as she mounted the steps to the library, when a movement out of the corner of my eye caught my attention. Turning, I saw Luke Bizzy a few yards down the sidewalk.

"You coming?" Doris turned back to see what was keeping me, then followed my line of sight. Doris gave Luke a jaunty little wave, then hustled me inside.

Gravestone Community Library was small, smelled like mothballs and dust, and was packed to the rafters with books.

"Y'all need a bigger library," I said, eyeing the double stacked bookshelves to my right.

"The school uses it too," Doris explained. "Since the school isn't big enough to warrant their own library. So, this place ends up with all the books required for their various curriculums, and then, of course, when someone passes on, their collection of books finds its way here."

I thought about all the books I'd boxed up from John's house and had done exactly that.

"Why don't they stop accepting donations, then?"

"A library? Turn away books? Don't be absurd." The voice came from behind a pile of books stacked one atop the other until they had to be over six feet tall.

"Ah, Ida, can you point us to the historical section?" Doris asked the stack of books.

"Romance?" the voice—I assumed it belonged to Ida—asked.

Doris snorted. "Town history."

"You want aisle three, sixth shelf on your left."

Despite there not being any signs identifying the aisles, Doris found her way and there we were, aisle three, sixth shelf on the left. One row of books depicted Gravestone's history.

"Slim pickings." I ran my fingers over the titles.

"Small town," Doris replied, pulling three books off the shelf and shoving them into my arms. "Make a start on these." Doris pulled more titles from the shelf and squeezed past me to where two desks sat at the back of the room. There was hardly enough space to swing a cat, let alone sit and study. Before I could follow, a strange sensation overtook me, like invisible fingers weaving magic.

Swiveling on my heel, I put the books back on the shelf and closed my eyes, doing my best to clear my mind. Hard to do when it's full of holes and confusion, but I wanted to follow that magic, find its source, for it felt like it was calling my name, trying to get my attention. Cracking open one eye, I saw it, golden fairy dust leaving a sparkling path from where I was standing to the bottom shelf two book cases away.

Of course, I followed the trail. Kneeling in front of the bookcase, I ran my hands over the spines of the leather-bound books, feeling the power and emotion of their stories as my fingers brushed over them. I gasped and snatched my hand away, gulping in a breath, before tentatively reaching out again, drawn to the power. This was new. My magic had never done this before, and despite being ordered not to use it, I was in too deep to turn back now.

Then I found it, nestled between the thick tomes, the book I was meant to find. Clasping the spine, I tugged it from its resting place, magical particles dancing above the book like a thousand fireflies before dissolving into nothing but air. There was no title on the cover, no author, nothing but old, supple leather and a decorative swirl etched into each corner.

Laying it on my knees, I carefully opened it. The first few pages were blank, and I thought I'd been tricked and this was nothing but a ruse, but on the third page was one word. Marilla. The name of the woman in the statue in the town square.

Turning the page, I began to read. It was the love story of Marilla, the mermaid, and her human lover Captain George Chauncey, who loved her so much he named his ship after her and would count the days until he'd sail into the shores of Gravestone to be with his love once more. When Marilla fell pregnant, he was overjoyed, but when the babe was born, he learned the secret Marilla had kept from him all this time. She was a mermaid, and the offspring of a mermaid was born a seal. Repulsed, he scorned Marilla and the child she named Earendil, throwing them overboard and assuming they'd perish at sea.

I paused, my hand flat on the page. George couldn't have been the sharpest tool in the shed if he thought throwing a mermaid and a seal into the ocean would kill them. Maybe Marilla was well rid of him. Shaking my head, I returned to reading.

Marilla did not perish. Instead, she hid her baby in Gravestone's mangroves before returning to the ship, intent on slaughtering all on board, only to discover the crew were already dead, including George. Their bodies were drained of life, turned to mere husks.

"Mummies," I whispered, intrigued by this turn of events. Who, or what, had killed them?

Seemed Marilla had the same question, for she searched the ship for answers. She found it below deck, in the captain's cabin. An open chest sat in the middle of the room. Inside the chest, a lone object nestled with a leather pouch.

My heart beat faster, and I held my breath because I knew what was coming. This had to be what we were searching for. Why else would I have been led to this book?

Scooping up the pouch, Marilla tipped the contents into her hand. It was an amulet on a leather cord. And within the amulet, magic as old as time itself. Magic that had stolen the souls of the humans who'd dared to open the chest. The Shadowfall Amulet.

I gasped out loud, clapping a hand over my mouth to stifle the sound. A quick glance over my shoulder showed Doris hadn't heard, blissfully unaware of what I'd discovered. Returning to the book, I read on.

Returning the amulet to its pouch, she secured the strings over her wrist, and before she left the ship for the final time, she lit a torch and tossed it onto the deck, waiting until the flames took hold before diving overboard, then watching from the ocean as the ship burned. With the pouch secured to her wrist, she returned to the mangroves and baby Earendil, vowing to destroy any and all ships that crossed her path from this point forward. All sailors would suffer for George's treatment of her.

"Wait," I whispered, pausing once more. "So, baby Earendil wasn't murdered for seal meat? He lived? And the mermaids luring sailors to their deaths was Marilla, seeking revenge for being scorned by George? I mean, there's vengeance and then there's vengeance." I wasn't sure whether to be impressed or horrified. Remaining undecided, I returned to the story.

Earendil did indeed survive. And Marilla lived

another forty years, wreaking her fury at being betrayed by the human she loved until she was too old and frail to do so. To protect his mother from the humans hunting them, Earendil spun a web of lies, how the mermaid Marilla's newborn was killed and the mermaids, in their horror and anger, took to the seas, vowing retribution by luring seamen to their deaths.

When Marilla passed away, Earendil laid her to rest in a private tomb beneath Gravestone, and with her, her most treasured possession. The Shadowfall Amulet.

Silently, I closed the book. Somewhere beneath Gravestone was a tomb, in that tomb a coffin, and in that coffin, the Shadowfall Amulet. Sliding the book back onto the shelf, I opened my mouth to tell Doris when the golden magic dust returned, swirled around the book, only to dissolve with a whisper soft pop.

I blinked, not sure I could trust what I was seeing, for the ancient tome with no title had been replaced by a book called *Pearl Hunting in the Persian Gulf*. A quick flick through the pages confirmed the story of Marilla was gone. But I'd seen it, read it, and knew the truth. A truth that apparently was meant for me and me alone.

Climbing to my feet, I dusted off my rear, cast another glance at Doris, and left the library. Outside, the storm clouds gathered, thunder rumbled, but no rain fell, just the oppressive heat and humidity and impending sense of doom.

CHAPTER FOURTEEN

Standing on the sidewalk, I was lost in thought when Luke Bizzy stepped into my path, blocking my way.

"Tess." His voice was a deep rumble, like he'd spent his life drinking whiskey and smoking cigars.

"What do you want?" I studied him, taking in the stubble, the crows' feet at the corners of his eyes, and the frown lines between his brows. A baseball cap pulled low over his brow shaded his eyes. Were they brown or hazel or something in between?

He looked at me for a moment, then held out his hand. "Luke Bizzy."

"I know who you are. And I know you know me. You're SIA." Then that darned knife through the eyeball thing returned, and my words fell into a warbled cry of agony. Clutching my head, I doubled over. Luke wrapped an arm around my shoulders and guided me off the sidewalk, seeking shelter beneath the canopy of a tree, its huge trunk hiding us from prying eyes.

"I see your memories are returning," he said, making sure I was leaning against the trunk and not about to topple over before releasing his hold.

I squinted at him, my head threatening to explode. "What?"

"The pain you're feeling right now? That's the hex unraveling."

"It is?" I gasped, my eyes watering and blurring as the headache continued, ferocious and unrelenting. "Who put it on me? The SIA? And why did they send you?"

He inclined his head. "The coven thought it would keep you safe, but it's not holding. I warned them this would happen."

Pinching the bridge of my nose, I sucked in a deep breath. "I'm confused," I admitted. "What coven? Did Harding send you?" One minute we were talking about the SIA, the next some coven.

"Of course. You don't remember." He slapped his forehead. "Scott Harding is the name of the SIA's coven of witches."

"She'll snap out of it soon," Doris said, her voice echoing in my head. "She's had a big day. Lots of surprises."

"I didn't mean to break her," Luke replied. At the news that Harding wasn't a person but was, in fact, a coven of witches, my brain had melted. Shut down. Closed for business.

Luke and Doris hustled me into Doris's car, and if I hadn't been in a fugue state, I would have taken a moment to ask how Doris had found me. I'd left her in the library. Had Luke ducked inside to get her? But my world, as I knew it, was unraveling at an astonishing rate, and I was struggling to keep up. As we zipped through town, the fog lifted somewhat, and I pieced things together the best I could.

The Harding coven had hexed me. They'd been the ones to alter my memories. They sent me to Gravestone. And it was all related to the Shadowfall Amulet. It had to be.

"Here we are, home sweet home," Doris said, turning to look at me where I was splayed across the back seat of the Impala.

Luke, riding shotgun, slung an arm over the back of the seat, and looked at me. "Feeling better?"

"Much." Climbing out of the car, I slammed the door behind me with more force than necessary.

"Well, if you ladies are okay, I'll head off." Luke stood beside Doris's car, intent on leaving. He must've come with Doris on the off chance she needed a hand getting me inside, but since I was up and mobile, he was keen to leave.

"Nuh-uh." I waggled a finger in his face. "Oh, no you don't. Inside." I pointed to the front door. "We're not done here."

Luke looked at Doris, who said, "Best do as she says, son. She's in a bit of a mood today."

"A bit of a mood?" I practically yelled. "You try finding out everything you think you know is one big fat lie and see if that doesn't put you in a *bit of a mood.*"

"Okay, okay, geez," Doris grumbled, leading the way down the garden path. "Don't get your panties in a wad."

"Sorry." I trailed behind, casting glances to the left and right. I couldn't shake the feeling I was being watched, yet other than us, there wasn't another soul on Berryman Street. Correction, there wasn't another soul that I could see. That didn't mean someone wasn't hiding. Watching. Waiting.

Once inside, Doris headed for the coffeepot

while I sat at the kitchen table. I pointed to the chair opposite, and Luke obediently sat.

"Tell me about the Shadowfall Amulet. That is why you're here, isn't it?"

He inclined his head. "Actually, Tess—"

"Holly," Doris and I corrected.

"Actually, *Holly*, you were the one who discovered the connection."

"Connection?"

Luke cast a glance at Doris. "I figured with an SIA agent involved, you'd put the pieces together pretty fast. Harding didn't factor that in."

"What are you even talking about?" He may as well have been speaking in riddles for all the sense he was making.

Crossing his arms, Luke leaned back in his seat and said in a monotone, "There is an ancient coven called the Shadow Binder Covenant, thought to be extinct, but it turns out there's a handful of witches trying to resurrect the coven and all that it stands for." He paused to take a breath. "I can tell by your faces that this isn't news to you."

We nodded.

"And the one and only purpose of the Covenant is to open the Obsidian Field, which is basically the veil between our world and another. In this case, they want to drop the veil to release the Draughr's."

"Witch vampire hybrids," Doris said. "But they aren't real."

"Oh, they exist," Luke told her. "Just not in our dimension. And of course, it's SIA's job to keep it that way."

"We read in John Smith's journal that you need both the Codex of the Solstice and the Shadowfall Amulet to open the Obsidian Field," I said.

"And the witch who cast the spell."

I frowned. "What spell?"

"The spell that turned the Codex and the Amulet into a lock and key."

"Was John Smith that witch?" Doris asked hopefully, but Luke shook his head.

"John was a gatekeeper. His death left the gates unattended. The SIA is still scrambling to find a replacement, although technically, it's not their role to do so."

"What gates? You're not talking about the gates of Hell, are you?" If so, things were going from bad to worse. Hell was a whole other dimension you didn't want anyone messing with.

"No, the gates to Purgatory."

I sagged in relief. "You're telling me John Smith

guarded the gates to *Purgatory?* The realm between Heaven and Hell?"

"Correct. Initially, we thought his death was a targeted attack, an attempt to breech the gates, but we've since discovered that isn't the case. His death was an unfortunate incident, and the witch who managed to get under his radar and hex him had no idea of his true identity."

"And what does it mean now that John is dead and the gates are unguarded? Can the souls get out?" Doris asked.

"Purgatory is in lockdown. No one in or out. Not until we can install a new gatekeeper."

"Why the delay?"

"Because the gatekeeper needs a certain set of skills, and it takes time to recruit. A gatekeeper has never been murdered before." He paused. "You haven't asked the obvious question."

"The witch," Doris piped up, sliding a cup of coffee in front of me, another in front of Luke. "The witch who cast the original spell, who clearly can't still be alive because we're talking hundreds of years ago. Right?"

"Correct. They need a witch from the same bloodline." And he looked at me.

The sense of impending doom increased a

thousandfold, settling like a wet, heavy blanket on my shoulders. "Please don't tell me I'm that witch."

Turned out Luke's eyes were not brown or hazel. They were cold, gray, and expressionless and didn't waver. "You're that witch."

"Is this why I'm here? In Gravestone? It's got nothing to do with some counterfeit wand smuggling ring, does it? Why not just tell me the truth?"

"The truth is dangerous."

"So what? You thought it would be a good idea to keep me safe by busting my foot and erasing my memories? Geez, thanks, don't do a girl any favors, will you?"

"Holly, love, calm down." Doris lay a soothing hand on my shoulder. "It's all going to be okay."

"How can it be?" I brushed her hand away, irritated and exhausted at the games others had been playing with my life. "I don't know who I am, but apparently, I have this big secret destiny that others would kill to stop me from fulfilling, because that's the truth of it, right Luke? That's the whole reason Harding messed with my head."

He regarded me coldly, not one ounce of compassion on his face. "None of that is important right now. What is important is finding the

Shadowfall Amulet before it falls into the wrong hands."

"You know what this means?" Doris clapped her hands together and bounced up and down.

"What does it mean, Doris?" I sighed.

"That there's a treasure hunt within the treasure hunt!"

Luke and I looked at her. Me with surprise, Luke with a smattering of admiration that dissipated as quickly as it had appeared. "One would think the treasure hunt was manufactured for this very reason," he said.

I snapped my fingers. "That's why Dino came back." Finally, something I understood. "He was searching for the Amulet."

"Uh yeah, only one problem. Someone killed him before he found it," Doris pointed out.

"But what if he did find it? What if that's why he was murdered?"

Luke narrowed his eyes. "You think Cittadino had the Amulet in his possession when he died?"

"It makes sense, doesn't it? As far as motives go?"

The sound of little paws scampering across the floor caught my attention. Looking over Luke's shoulder, I pointed a finger at Flynn. "And you!" He froze in his tracks at my raised voice and cautiously turned his head. "I'm not one hundred percent certain you're Gavin Flynn. Which begs the question… who are you?"

He stared at me for a second longer, as if digesting what I'd said, then stood on his hind legs and proceeded to squeak up a storm. An angry storm by the sounds of things. And while I couldn't understand him, I most certainly understood his parting gesture. He flipped me the bird.

Doris roared with laughter while I sat watching his departing rear and flicking tail with my mouth hanging open. I turned to Doris, needing confirmation of what I'd just witnessed. "Did he?"

"He most certainly did," she chortled, wiping her eyes. "I think you can safely assume he took offense to that."

"Maybe he's Flynn after all." Because that was certainly something he'd do.

"That's Flynn," Luke confirmed.

Now I felt like all kinds of a heel for doubting him. "How come he's a rat then? If the whole counterfeit wand thing didn't happen, how did I get hurt and Flynn got changed into a rat?"

"Flynn is the one who put the Algiz protection rune on you." Luke nodded toward the rune on my collarbone. "After you were attacked."

"Wait, what?"

"He's a sorcerer." Luke shrugged.

"Then why can't he change out of rat form?" Doris demanded.

"Because he was hexed. As soon as he used his magic, he was transformed into a rat. He knew it would happen, but he did it anyway. To protect you."

"He did?" I couldn't hide the wobble in my voice.

"He was the one who worked out your bloodline. That you were a descendant of the witch who cast the original spell. Only someone else found out too and tried to snatch you. That's how you broke your foot. It was after that failed attempt that Flynn put the protection spell on you and Harding wiped your mind. Then the SIA sent you here. And since Flynn was stuck in rat form, they sent him with you."

"And Kerris Jones? Where does she fit in all of this?"

Luke's brows shot up. "The mayor? She's a person of interest. She's a known associate of the Tarkath Syndicate. We keep tabs on her."

"She's a witch, isn't she?" Doris chimed in. "Tell me she's a witch."

Luke shook his head. "Nope, not a witch."

"Darn."

"And the sheriff? How does Calder factor in?"

"Calder is one of our best assets. He does an excellent job of serving the human population while also keeping an eye on all things paranormal."

"What I don't get is that if Gravestone is such a hotbed of paranormal activity, why not station an SIA agent here permanently?"

Luke shrugged. "Above my paygrade. My best guess is that the director doesn't see the need, what with the work Calder does for us and having a retired agent living here. Now." Luke stood. "If you'll excuse me, I have an amulet to find."

I shot to my feet. "Wait."

I didn't miss the look of annoyance that flashed across his face.

"I'm coming with you. *We're* coming with you," I amended, pointing to Doris and me.

"I work alone." Luke continued to the front door, and I hurried behind.

"You're SIA. You've worked with partners before," I protested. "Plus, we already have something you're going to need."

"Holly," Doris warned.

Luke shot me a curious look over his shoulder. "Oh, yeah? And what's that?"

"The Codex of the Solstice."

You could have heard a pin drop, the silence was

that loud. Doris tugged on the back of my shirt, and I turned to look at her. Her eyes were wide, and she had a finger up to her lips. *Shh.*

"You have it?" One thing about Luke Bizzy—he was a calm, levelheaded individual and despite telling him we already had one part of the magical lock and key everyone was searching for, he didn't show an ounce of surprise.

"I know where it is," I hedged, heeding Doris's warning. Something had spooked her, to warn me to keep quiet about the Codex. But what neither of them knew was that I knew where the Amulet was. Thanks to the book of Marilla, I knew exactly where to go. Well... kind of. I had no idea there were caves beneath Gravestone, but once I found them, I was convinced we'd find Marilla's tomb and the Amulet.

Someone pounded on the front door, and we all jumped. Except for Luke, who remained stoic and steadfast.

"It'll be another one of those treasure hunters," I grumbled, pushing him aside to fling open the door. Only it wasn't a treasure hunter.

"Sheriff," I greeted Calder, ignoring my traitorous heart that picked up a jaunty new rhythm at the sight of him.

His gaze swept over all of us before coming back to me. "The gang's all here."

"We're just heading out." I couldn't keep the frost out of my voice. I was still smarting and, despite knowing I was being utterly ridiculous, my emotions were having none of it. They were going to remain annoyed until they were good and ready to forgive.

"Holly, we need to talk."

"We'll give you a minute," Doris chimed in, grabbing Luke's arm and dragging him toward the kitchen.

"Hey," he protested. "I told you I work alone. And I'm outta here."

"Two minutes won't kill you."

I stepped out, closing the door behind me, leaving Doris and Luke bickering inside.

"You heard her. You've got two minutes," I said.

Calder didn't beat around the bush. Lifting his hand, he stroked his thumb along my cheek. I practically melted into a puddle at his feet.

"I'm sorry." Two simple little words that hold the weight of the world. Probably more powerful than I love you. Calder's voice was all low and grumbly. "I'm sorry if you think I lied to you."

Think? I snorted, jerking away from his caress. He

shoulda quit while he was ahead and left it at the apology. "You did."

He shook his head. "I just didn't tell you what I knew."

"You lied by omission."

"I was doing my job."

I studied him through narrowed eyes, not wanting to admit he had a point. Harding had hidden me here, memories altered, with a bounty on my head and instructions for Calder to keep an eye on me. And he'd done exactly that. Why, then, was I so mad about it? If our roles had been reversed, I'd have done exactly the same thing. *Because you like him. And after that kiss on my porch, maybe he likes me too?*

"What's Luke doing here?"

His question took me by surprise.

"Why? Jealous?" Oh my goodness, but I needed to send an urgent message to my mouth to shut the hell up!

Calder moved in close, trapping me between the door and his tall, hot, muscular body. "Do I need to be?" His growl sent a shiver right down to my toes. "Because I can do that. For you."

With his mouth a scant inch from mine, I squeaked the first response that popped into my head. "What?" *So eloquent, Holly. That's the best you got?*

Words would not be my savior in this situation, so I did the next best thing. Throwing my arms around his neck, I pulled his mouth down to mine and kissed him. He was molten fire that threatened to consume my very soul, and I abandoned myself to it, riding the waves, knowing in every fiber of my being that I could trust this bear of a man who had me wrapped in his arms. Arms that could crush but instead cradled me so gently. And that's when I heard it echoing through my mind. I could trust him. Joshua Calder was a man I could trust with all my heart.

Tearing my mouth from his, I cupped his face in my hands and whispered, "I can trust you."

"You can." His panty-melting growl was my undoing, and I had visions of ripping his clothes off then and there when a bang on the other side of the door doused my overheated fantasies. I'd forgotten we had company.

"I'm not hearing any talking," Doris yelled through the door. "So, I'm assuming you've made up. Or are making out?"

My face burned with embarrassment, while

Calder chuckled and pulled me closer, letting me bury my overheated face against his chest.

"Give us a second," he called. Then, with his mouth against my ear, he said, "Quick. Fill me in. What's Luke doing here?"

Tilting my head back, I basked in the reassurance of his embrace. "I had another headache. Luke told me it was the hex that had altered my memories coming unraveled. He and Doris brought me home."

Calder lowered his head to rest his forehead against mine. "I'm glad they kept you safe. How are you feeling now?"

"I'm fine. It wasn't as bad as last time. But something else happened that I haven't told Doris or Luke about." I chewed my lip, worried he was going to think I was nuts when I told him about the magic book, but to his credit, he kept a straight face and accepted everything I said.

"I know where the caves are," he said.

"You *believe* me?"

He smiled and touched my cheek. "Of course I believe you. Out of all of this, why would you lie? Okay, fine, let's not count the fact that you've been lying to me on a daily basis since you arrived." He softened the accusation with a wink.

"Fine," I huffed. "I get the hint. I've got no right to

be mad at you about a few lies when I've done nothing but lie. I get it." In my defense, I was lying to protect my cover. I didn't know I could trust him.

"I think we can both agree that these are exceptional circumstances and that all lies are forgiven. But from this point onward, we're honest with each other. Agreed?" he said.

Stretching onto tip-toes, I planted a quick, hard kiss on his lips. "Agreed."

The doorknob turned. Doris was done waiting, and she was coming out. Calder swept me out of the way, and as he did so, he whispered in my ear, "Don't mention the book. Follow my lead."

"How goes it, Calder?" Doris beamed at us, her eyes darting from my heated face to Calder's grin. She didn't miss a thing, but rather than embarrassing me further, she gave a satisfied nod.

Luke followed her out, his eyes narrowing. "Sheriff. I'm assuming your visit is for personal reasons?"

I stiffened. How was Calder's visit any of Luke's business? But Calder, with his arm still around my shoulders, gave me a slight squeeze, warning me— presumably—that he had this all under control, so I kept my mouth shut.

"Business and pleasure," Calder said. "Holly and I

needed to talk, and I have a lead. I figured I could kill two birds with one stone and take her with me."

"A lead?" Doris was all over it, tossing the Impala keys in the air and catching them with one hand. "Let's go."

"What's the lead?" Luke asked, body alert.

"The caves. We have reason to believe Dino was killed over some artifact that may or may not be hidden in the caves." Calder squeezed me again, warning me not to say anything. I nudged him in the ribs. As if he had to remind me.

Doris's mouth rounded into a perfect O. "The caves! That's brilliant! What better place to hide treasure than in a pirate's cave? Man, I wish I'd thought of that."

"Who's your source?" Luke asked.

Calder shook his head. "I came by to ask for volunteers—the caves are vast and too big for one person to search—but I can't reveal my source."

Luke's chest puffed out as he squared off. "You are aware I'm SIA. I out rank you."

"Yeah, but I'm the sheriff of this town, and what I say goes. And I say I'm not revealing my source. I'm investigating a murder, and while I appreciate you're in Gravestone on some sort of mission, it's definitely not to find out who killed Dino Cittadino. So, I'm not revealing my source. You got a problem with that?"

Doris grabbed me by the wrist and tugged me down the steps, whispering in my ear, "You see what we have here folks," she mimicked in her best David Attenborough voice, "is our typical male posturing situation. Whose johnson is the biggest? We'll just have to wait and see. Maybe they'll whip 'em out and measure 'em." She dropped the pretense and said in her normal voice, "You know, I've often wondered that. I mean, do men really measure their appendages? And if so, what's the unit of measurement because six inches isn't the six inches my measuring tape tells me it is?"

I burst out laughing and both men turned to look, Calder's eyes dancing with amusement, Luke's burning with anger. *Oh boy*. Searching the caves was going to be fun with a capital F with these two alpha males.

CHAPTER FIFTEEN

Doris, Flynn, and I rode in the Impala so I could fill Doris in on the important stuff—AKA, the kiss with Calder—while Luke caught a ride with the sheriff.

"Aww, it's so sweet." Doris sighed, peering through the gap between the steering wheel and dashboard. "Young love."

"I'd hardly call us young. More like middle-aged love. And it's not love." *Lust, most definitely.*

"Give it time."

And that brought me to my next problem. Time. I didn't know how long I'd be in Gravestone. As soon as we found the Shadowfall Amulet, the case would be closed. SIA would lock it in the vault at HQ, along with the Codex that was still hiding out in my elm tree. There'd be no reason for me to be hiding out anymore. The threat would be over. There was no wand heist, no bounty on my head— well, not the type of bounty I'd thought. I was only in danger because I was related to the witch who'd cast the original spell, and without the Amulet and Codex, I was of no use to anyone.

"You've gone quiet," Doris said, navigating the narrow gravel road that took us out to the headland and the caves of Gravestone.

"I'm wondering what my role in this is," I said. "Just because I'm related to the witch who cast a spell centuries ago doesn't mean I know the spell required to unlock… whatever it is. I mean, I assume that's what the Codex and Amulet are for… the lock and the key. Why do they need a witch?"

Flynn, riding on my shoulder, squeaked and tugged on my hair. Reaching up, I plucked him from my shoulder and cradled him in my hand so I could see him. "What? You know something?"

He squeaked and nodded.

"What is it? What do they need me for?"

Then he bit me. The little rat bastard bit me. "Ow! Flynn, what the hell?" I dropped him on my lap, reaching for a tissue from the box Doris had wedged in the center console to wipe at the drop of blood that had formed.

"That's it!" Doris cried, practically running us off the road.

"Doris!" I screamed. "Eyes on the road."

She jerked the wheel, getting us back on track. "Sorry, sorry. But that's it. That's what Flynn is trying to tell you. They need your blood."

Lifting the tissue with my blood smeared across it, I realized she was right. Flynn was right.

"*Of course*. I said it before, this is dark magic. Blood magic."

"So it makes perfect sense they want—*need*—your blood."

"Do you think the SIA knew that? When they sent me here? Because I can't help but feel like I've been served up on a platter."

"Walking into the lion's den," Doris agreed.

"But the SIA can't want the Obsidian Field opened. Can they?"

"And what about Dino? Where does he fit into all this? John's book mentioned nothing about a sacrifice."

"Maybe we don't have the full story? John wrote about what he knew, but what if there was more to discover?"

"Holy cockadoodles, but this is turning into an Agatha Christie novel." Doris shot me a cheeky grin. "I say, Watson old chap."

"That's not Agatha Christie." I chuckled. "That's Sherlock Holmes."

The track came to an abrupt end at a clearing big enough to park three cars, four at a squeeze. Doris pulled to a stop, and seconds later, Calder pulled up next to us. After the dust settled, we all climbed out, meeting at the back of Calder's truck.

"Flashlight," he said, handing each of us a flashlight. Then he handed Luke a radio. "We won't have cell reception in the caves."

Doris pushed to the front. "Where's mine?"

"We'll be searching in pairs," Calder told her. "You'll be with Luke. Holly will be with me."

"Let's go." Luke was two strides ahead, leading the way to a roughly beaten path that snaked down a steep embankment leading to the beach.

"Do you even know where you're going, hotshot?" Doris trotted behind him.

"How hard can it be? We're on top of a bluff looking for caves. Here's a path. Ergo, follow the path that will take us to the beach where I'm assuming the caves are."

"Smarty pants."

I looked at Calder, who shrugged. "He's not wrong."

Without another word, I followed, with Calder bringing up the rear. It was tough going in a walking boot. I'd expected Flynn to run ahead, but he stayed on my shoulder, gripping my hair and trying to maintain his balance with every slip and slide as I grappled with the uneven terrain.

"Did Dino's autopsy results come back yet?" My slow going meant we'd lost sight of Doris and Luke. I figured it was safe to ask.

"Actually, yes, and it revealed something interesting."

"Oh?"

"Dino had a freshly inked tattoo."

"I don't see the relevance," I admitted. "Dino had several tattoos. What's one more?"

"It was right where his chest was cut open."

"As in X marks the spot?" I suggested.

Calder nodded. "And so recent there was still tattoo powder on his skin."

"Tattoo powder? Not ink?" Was that the red powder I'd found on Dino's chest?

"Forensics tested the powder and confirmed it was pigment powder, but the tattoo itself, well the parts of it that weren't destroyed by his... injury...

also contained witch hazel, glycerin, and propylene glycol."

"I'm guessing that's what's in tattoo ink?"

"Homemade tattoo ink."

"Must be a messy tattoo artist if they got the powder all over him. You'd have to mix the ink up in some sort of container first, right? Not directly on the skin."

"I'm no tattoo expert, but yeah, I would think you'd create your ink before you start."

"You know who does know about tattoos? Fay Tality. She was a tattoo artist before she got into this whole social media influencer thing. You should ask her about it."

"Noted."

"And?" I prompted, knowing there was more. "Was his heart missing?"

"Affirmative."

Before we could discuss the ramifications of what that meant, I lost my footing and slipped, arms flailing. Calder grabbed me, keeping a firm hold as we slid the last few feet of the path. The downward trajectory was steep, and I was already worrying about how I was going to climb back up.

We eventually reached the beach, which wasn't the golden sand I'd been expecting. In fact, there wasn't a grain of sand to be seen. It was all rocks and seaweed. Doris and Luke were specks in the distance as they made their way to the base of the overhanging cliffs lining the horseshoe bay.

"I can see why the path is rubbish," I puffed, sweating profusely from our trek. "Not exactly a tourist attraction."

"They say Seal Cove is the perfect spot for boats to wait out passing storms," Calder said. "And not much else. Although the locals claim the fishing isn't bad. You can throw in a line from the rocks."

I looked at the cliffs, then at Calder. "I can't make it. Not with this." I pointed to my walking boot. The path had been bad enough, but clambering over rocks and boulders? No chance.

"I'll piggy back you," Calder said, already turning to offer me his back.

Chewing my lip, I tentatively placed my hands on his shoulders while he bent his knees so I could jump on board. "Are you sure? I'm heavier than I look."

"It's fine. I'm a bear, remember?"

"Oh, well, since you put it that way." I launched onto his back, and he staggered forward while simultaneously looping his arms around my legs. Flynn squeaked in protest and launched off my shoulder, sailing through the air to land on a rock a few feet away before scampering to join Doris and Luke.

Calder covered the uneven ground to the base of the cliffs with ease, as if he didn't have extra pounds clinging to his back. He nimbly stepped from one rock to another until he lowered me to the ground at the opening of the cave.

"I wasn't expecting it to be this big," I said, eyeing the yawning opening carved into the rocks that had to be at least two stories high.

"It's deceiving," Calder said. "The opening is huge, but it gets small fast. Hope you're not claustrophobic."

"That would have been something to mention when we were at the top," I groaned, and Calder froze, staring at me.

"Oh God, you're not, are you?"

The silence stretched on for several seconds before I giggled. "Gotcha."

Doris made a guffaw sound and slapped Calder on the back. "She got you there."

He shook his head, but I saw the smirk curling his lips before he reached into his pockets, pulling out two Zip-lock bags and handing one to me and one to Doris. "Glow sticks to mark your trail, so we can find our way out."

The main entry of the cave had been vandalized over the years, graffiti tags spray painted on the walls, but the deeper we moved, the darker it got, and the remnants of campfires and signs of graffiti soon disappeared. As Calder predicted, the cave got narrower and lower until the roof was almost brushing the top of my head. It was at that point it branched off into two tunnels.

"We'll take the left," Calder said. "You take the right. Radio if you find anything."

"What was this tip off you got anyway?" Luke asked. "So we know what we're searching for. I doubt the Amulet is sitting on some sort of pedestal with a heavenly beam shining down on it saying *here I am*."

"A burial site," Calder replied. "Old. Ancient."

"Are you telling me someone has been buried down here all this time and no one knows?" Doris sounded shocked at the very thought of it.

"Not anyone in our lifetime, Doris," Calder said, somewhat cryptically.

"Is it the original witch?" Her guess wasn't that far off. But Marella wasn't the original witch. She was a lovesick mermaid who'd taken her broken heart out on poor, innocent sailors.

Calder ignored her question. "Holly?"

"I'm ready," I told him. "Flynn, stay close."

The floor of the cave was unexpectedly smooth, unlike the rocky shore, so I was able to limp along behind Calder, our footsteps echoing down the narrow tunnel.

"You've been here before, right?" I asked, doing my best to hide the nervous tremor in my voice. "You know your way around the caves?"

I'd tossed one glow stick a few feet in, but since the tunnel hadn't branched off in any other direction yet, there was no point dropping more. Unless my flashlight gave out, then I'd be snapping these puppies and the caves would glow like Christmas.

"Yeah, I've been down here a few times. Never came across a coffin, though."

"You don't think it's real?"

"I think you were shown the book for a reason. Marella's story was revealed to you, and you alone. Why? I have no idea, but I say let's roll with it, see where it takes us."

"You're taking all of this remarkably well."

"You forget that I'm not human. You think I haven't seen some crazy things in the shifter world?"

"Why do you keep that a secret, anyway? That you're a bear shifter," I clarified.

"It suits my purposes not to have it be common knowledge. As far as the townsfolk are concerned, I'm as human as they come. Does that mean they let their guard down, think I won't notice an anomaly or two? Maybe."

"Ha!" I barked out a laugh that echoed loudly all around us, making me jump. Even Flynn squeaked. In a whisper, I added, "Smart. Luke says you work with the SIA regularly."

He shrugged. "From time to time, sure. I keep an eye on things, but my main role is sheriff of Gravestone. Keeping humans safe is my top priority."

"Same as the SIA."

"Yes, and no. The Supernatural Investigation Agency was created to keep rogue paranormals in line. To bring them to justice for crimes they commit. Sometimes that involves the human world, sometimes it doesn't."

"And did you know, when Harding called, that I was a witch? Speaking of, did you know that Scott Harding isn't a he? It's a coven. The SIA's coven."

Calder stopped and turned to look at me. I

couldn't read his face, hidden by the shadows. "Harding is a *coven?*"

"You didn't know?"

"I always spoke with a man who introduced himself as Scott Harding." He paused, then added, "And no, I didn't know you were a witch. Obviously, you were something, otherwise the SIA wouldn't have sent you here to hide out."

"So, it was no coincidence you were on that road the day I arrived."

"Actually, it was. Hector should never have dropped you off where he did. His job is to drive passengers all the way into town, so I was keeping an eye on the town square—where you should have gotten off. Since he hadn't turned up, I thought I'd go check the state of the road since it was all torn up. Figured he may have run into trouble with the bus and needed a hand."

The radio clipped to Calder's belt crackled, and I could just make out a garbled message dispersed with static.

Calder held the radio to his mouth and pressed the button. "Bizzy? You there? Over." Releasing the button, he waited for a response, but all we got was the same garbled voice and more static.

"Seems the radios don't work in the caves either," I said.

"Which is odd because I've used them down here before, on other search and rescue missions, and they worked fine."

"People have been lost down here before?" I did my best to hide the panic the thought of being trapped underground brought out in me, but Calder saw right through me.

"Drunk teenagers, mostly. It's fine. You're with me."

CHAPTER SIXTEEN

"Come on, let's keep going. I've searched these caves before and there's only one area I've never explored."

"Why not?"

"It's difficult to get to."

I'd already had a bad feeling. Calder's words added to it, and the sense of doom that had been dogging my heels for days was reaching unbearable proportions. I felt like screaming just to break the tension.

The caves were a veritable labyrinth, and I was dropping glow sticks frequently. That, at least, gave me some comfort that we'd be able to find our way out. That and the map Calder had on his phone.

"I thought you said there's no reception down here?"

"There isn't. This is downloaded." The glow from the screen briefly illuminated his face as he wiggled his phone. He wasn't worried. He was calm. In fact— I cocked my head as I studied him—I'd even say he was having fun.

"Do you think Marilla is really buried down here?" I asked, as we resumed the journey forward. "Is the story of Marilla even real? Did she ever exist?"

"You're thinking it's just some folk story? A fairy tale?"

"It does seem farfetched."

"We know mermaids exist," Calder said, while consulting the map on his phone and taking a sharp right. "So, it wouldn't be beyond the realm of possibilities to find one buried here. Although it *does* surprise me that one is buried on land. I don't know a lot about merfolk lore, but I would have thought a burial at sea was the norm."

"Good point. Why did Earendil lay his mother to rest in the caves, rather than return her body to the ocean?" I paused for a moment, then answered my own question. "Because of the Shadowfall Amulet."

We walked in silence, the tunnels twisting and

turning, branching off and seeming to turn back on themselves. I was one hundred percent lost, but we had Calder's phone and the glow sticks. Flynn, who'd been trotting ahead of Calder as if he knew the way, stopped and stood up on his rear legs, nose lifted to sniff the air, whiskers twitching.

"What is it, Flynn?"

He squeaked a response, then took off running.

"Wait! Flynn!" My yell echoed around us as we hurried after the rodent, who was surprisingly fast given his ever-expanding girth. Flynn had been enjoying my baking a little too much.

We were falling behind because of me and my stupid walking boot. I shoved Calder in the back. "Go!" I urged. "Follow him. I'm right behind you."

"You sure?" Calder shot me a look over his shoulder, his expression a mixture of concern and intrigue. He was as curious as I was at what had gotten Flynn's attention.

"Follow him, and for all that is holy, do not lose him. If he gets lost down here, I'll never forgive myself."

Calder stopped long enough to press a hard kiss on my lips and then he was jogging after Flynn, leaving me standing there like a loon with a dopey grin on my face and my fingers tracing over the tingling his kiss had left behind.

Pulling myself together, I pushed forward, listening to the sounds of Calder's footsteps slowly fading. Soon it was silent, nothing but black in front of me, broken by the arc of my flashlight as it bounced over the rock walls looming on either side.

I needn't have worried about losing them. The tunnel came to a dead end, only at knee height, an opening. "You have got to be kidding me." Dropping to my hands and knees, I peered through the now significantly smaller tunnel. They had to have gone this way. There was nowhere else for them to have gone.

As I crawled inside, I thought about Doris and hoped she was having a better time of it. Then another thought hit me. What if Doris and Luke found Marilla's coffin and with the radios not working, they had no way of notifying us and we were crawling around in dark tunnels in a cave system that seemed to go on for miles deep beneath the earth, none the wiser?

I crawled faster, wincing as my kneecap came into contact with a sharp rock.

By the time I reached the cave that the tunnel led to, I was drenched in sweat. My breaths were coming in great gulps as I tried to push down the panic threatening to consume me. I'd been joking about being claustrophobic, but if I'd known I'd be crawling through a narrow tunnel in the dark on my own, I may have elected to wait outside.

A beam of light hit me right in the face, frying my retinas and leaving me blind. "Argh!" I yelled, flinging up my arm to shield my face.

"Sorry." Calder lowered the light, then hurried to help me to my feet. "Good grief, what happened to you?"

I looked down to where his flashlight illuminated my torn-up knees and the blood smeared all over my shins. Correction. One shin. My walking boot was now covered in a lovely combination of blood and dust, working its way beneath the Velcro bindings. I just knew it was going to rub and irritate my skin on the walk out.

"What happened to me? I'll tell you what happened to me." I was building up to a full head of steam. "My so-called rat protector ran off ahead, leaving me behind. And you went after him. So I was by myself, in the dark, crawling through tunnels wearing nothing remotely protective like a pair of jeans." I pointed to his jeans, dusty at the knees. "I'm in shorts and a T-shirt. I wasn't expecting to be *crawling*."

"You told me to go after him." Calder kept his cool despite my rising temper. "Otherwise, I would have stayed with you. If I thought for a second you were in any danger, I'd never have left your side."

"I might have gotten lost." I pouted, and he chuckled.

"Did you?" He knew full well that the tunnel hadn't branched off, so there was no way I could have gotten lost.

"That's not the point."

"Okay, you cantankerous—but gorgeous— female, come look what we found." Taking my hand, Calder led the way to a mound of rocks in the center of the cave we found ourselves in. Flynn was sitting atop the rocks, looking pleased with himself.

"What's this?"

"It's a burial mound."

"Oh." I nodded. Then, "Oooooh!"

"If you had to bury a body in the caves, it makes sense that you'd simply pile rocks on top of them, not try to dig through the cave floor into the rock itself."

I aimed my flashlight at the burial mound. I guessed it was wide enough and high enough to cover a body. How big were mermaids, anyway? I assumed human size, since when on land, they could walk among humans undetected.

"Just one minor problem," Calder said, directing my flashlight toward a particular rock. "Someone beat us to it."

"What?" Sure enough, rocks had been pulled away from one end of the mound and were now scattered around. Beneath what remained of the rubble, skeletal remains. "Marella, I presume."

"Look around her neck area. The vertebrae are misaligned." Calder pointed.

"Are you saying her neck was broken?" The book had said she'd died of old age—old for a mermaid living on land that is.

Calder snorted. "No. I'm saying she was probably buried wearing the amulet and whoever unburied her snatched it from her neck."

"Right. That makes more sense."

"I thought so."

My shoulders slumped. "So, this was all for nothing."

"Not necessarily." Calder slung his arm around my shoulders and pulled me into his side. "We've been toying with the theory that Dino had found the amulet and someone killed him for it."

"Yes, but we still don't know if it was Dino who found it. What if it was someone else? Why, then, would they kill Dino? This whole thing started with his murder, and now here we are, crawling around in caves, looking for ancient relics. I can't help but think we've gotten way off track."

"Maybe, maybe not. But there is one way to know if Dino was here."

"Oh? What's that?"

"His knees. If he crawled through that tunnel"—Calder's flashlight swung around the cave to the only opening leading to the chamber we were standing in to illustrate his point—"then there are bound to be bruises, maybe even scrapes like yours."

"Pft, I doubt he was wearing shorts."

"You're missing the point."

"No, I hear you. And you're right. Crawling on a rocky surface is bound to leave at least a mark of some sort. I assume if I inspect your knees, you'll have bruises forming?"

Calder smirked. "You trying to get me to take my pants off, babe?"

I don't know if it was the babe or the taking off the pants quip, but my face heated, and I totally lost my train of thought. Calder laughed. "Time for that later. Come on, let's get out of here. I need cell reception so I can call the coroner and have them check Dino's knees."

"Words I bet you never thought you'd say," I quipped, glad for the change of subject from his pants... or lack thereof.

The trek to the cave opening didn't take long, despite stopping to collect the glow sticks as we walked. Taking a seat on a rock just inside the cave, I closed my eyes and drew in a deep breath of salty fresh air while we waited for Doris and Luke. Calder kept trying the radio on the off-chance they'd hear his message—or at least realize he was trying to signal them—and return. Flynn flattened out on a rock next to me, belly up, snoring his head off.

"I'm going to go after them." Calder crouched by my side. "There's been no response on the radio, not even static. Something might have happened."

I craned my neck looking up at him. "It's odd, isn't it? That the radios aren't working?"

He ran a hand around the back of his neck and glanced back into the depths of the cave. "Yeah. Like I said, I've used them before. There's no reason they should suddenly stop working."

"Yoo-hoo!"

I'd never been so happy to hear Doris's voice. I'd had visions of her lost in the cave system, unable to find her way out. By the time I'd struggled to my feet, she'd reached us, Luke limping behind her.

"What happened?" I asked. "Calder was just about to come searching for you."

"This one twisted his ankle. I see you've added to your injury list." Doris pointed at my scraped knees.

"We had to crawl." I shrugged, like it was no big deal.

"And?" Doris asked, rubbing her hands together. "Did you find it?"

"We found where it *was*. Someone beat us to it."

"What?" Luke growled, clearly unimpressed with this piece of news. "Well, that's just great. No sense hanging around here any longer then, is there?"

"You got somewhere you need to be, hotshot?" Doris asked.

"As a matter of fact, I do." Luke's brow furrowed as he glanced at his watch. "The treasure hunt will be drawing to a close soon and the winner announced. I need to be there."

"Come on, then." Calder positioned himself in front of me. "Hop on."

He piggy backed me the entire way. While I'd had visions of having to haul myself up the slippery path to the headland on my hands and knees, he made it look easy, deftly making his way up the steep incline with what appeared to be little effort. Although by the time we reached the top, his breath was coming in heavy gasps and he'd worked up a sweat. Even so, I was impressed.

He then went back down to help Doris, who refused a piggy back but accepted a helping hand, then Luke, who was struggling with his twisted ankle. What a rag tag bunch we made. Eventually, we were all at the top.

"I'll drop you down at the shore, Luke. That's where the treasure hunt is wrapping up, right?"

"Yep. That'd be great, thanks." Luke limped toward Calder's truck while Calder turned to me, resting his hands on my shoulders. "I have some calls to make. You go get those knees cleaned up. I'll drop by later tonight."

"Don't tell me what to do," I protested weakly, distracted by his touch but unable to stop the automatic response to his order.

Calder smirked and held up his hands. "Fine," he teased. "Walk around looking like you've been kneecapped. Your choice."

"C'mon, Holly." Doris shoved me non-to-gently toward her Impala. "I need to pee." Piling into the car, we waited for Calder and Luke to leave and the dust to settle before following.

"Spill," Doris commanded. "What happened in the caves? Calder was cagey about his tip off."

"We were searching for Marilla's burial place. She had the amulet."

"Marilla? As in the mermaid Marilla? Whose statue is in the town square?"

"The one and only."

"I take it you found her? Calder said someone had beaten you to it."

"Yeah. It's hard to believe she's been down here all this time, undisturbed. But someone found her final resting place and tore the amulet from her neck."

Calder and I had repositioned the rocks on Marilla's grave before we left. It hadn't felt right to leave her exposed like that.

"So the question begs, who was Calder's snitch and how did they know about Marilla? And how in God's green gravy did Marilla come to have the Shadowfall Amulet?"

I squirmed in my seat. "I'd hardly call them a snitch," I protested. "It was a *lead*."

Doris shot me a shrewd look. "It was *you!*"

Flynn stirred in his sleep on my lap, rolling over and curling into a ball, his paws tucked in tight. It still made me unbearably sad to look at him, knowing he'd sacrificed his humanity to keep me safe. By using his magic to place the protection spell on me, he'd have known it would trigger his hex, but he'd done it, anyway. I just wish I could remember my relationship with him. It had to have been a strong one for him to do that for me.

"Holly Day." Doris snapped her fingers in front of my nose, drawing my attention.

"Watch the road, Doris!"

"I will if you'll tell me what in tarnation is going on."

"Fine, yes, I'm the lead. I had a vision. In the library, this book revealed itself to me. It was Marilla's story." I recounted what had happened to the mermaid, how her lover had attempted to kill her and her son. When she'd returned to the ship to exact her revenge, she'd discovered the entire crew dead, an open treasure chest, and inside the chest the Shadowfall Amulet.

"Wait," Doris frowned. "So, we're searching for an amulet that has the power to kill fifty men in one fell swoop?"

I shrugged. "I guess, potentially. I know as much as you."

"Maybe I don't want to find that thing after all."

She shuddered theatrically, and I couldn't help but smile. "Scared of a little old relic, Doris?" I teased.

"I'm a little old relic myself." Doris sniffed. "And I'd like to keep it that way, thanks very much. I'll shuffle off this mortal coil when I'm good and ready, and I'd prefer it wasn't at the hands of some old necklace."

The sun was low on the horizon when we entered the town limits, an orange ball blazing streams of light across the ocean, turning the sky a riot of pinks, purples, and reds.

"The sunsets here are really quite stunning," I said, shielding my eyes.

"They sure are," Doris agreed. "We'll swing by my place. I have a first aid kit."

I glanced at my knees. I'd already taken the skin off one when I'd come off the bicycle. Now I'd torn it up all over again, and I had to confess… it hurt. My knee throbbed in time with my heartbeat, and I quietly wondered if I'd done more damage than tearing off layers of flesh I couldn't afford to lose.

CHAPTER SEVENTEEN

Sitting at Doris's dining table, my legs extended on the chair opposite with an herbal poultice balanced on each kneecap, I flicked through the photos on Doris's camera. She'd snatched it from the back seat of the car before coming inside, muttering something about the memory card being full and that she needed to go through and dump a bunch of photos.

Flynn watched from his position on my shoulder as I scanned through photo after photo of Kerris.

"This is very stalkerish, Doris," I said, glancing up at the elderly woman who'd just returned from a shower.

"I prefer to call it investigating." She took a seat, rubbing at her damp hair with a towel. "Kerris Jones is up to her neck in something. It's just a matter of time before I find out what."

"Luke said the SIA is keeping an eye on her."

"Pft. What are they gonna do? She's human. She's out of their jurisdiction."

"But the people she's presumably hiring to do her dirty work aren't. Like Dino Cittadino. And we still don't know who killed him. We've come full circle, sitting at your dining room table trying to uncover the truth."

"Only last time, Fay was here. I wonder if she's learned anything new? Maybe I'll call her," Doris said.

"Good idea. I want to ask her about tattoos."

Doris's face lit up. "You thinking about getting some ink, Holly?"

"Nope. The coroner's report came in and Dino was sporting a fresh tattoo made with homemade ink. I wanted to ask her about it."

"You think *she* did the tattoo?" Doris's voice went up an octave.

"Nah, but she'd know where you'd buy the supplies, what you'd need, that type of thing. Unfortunately, the tattoo was on his chest and got messed up when the killer ripped his heart out, so we don't know if it's significant or not."

I was still blindly swiping the camera when Flynn squeaked and dug his claws into my shoulder, pointing.

"What's up?" I paused scrolling and brought the camera closer, squinting at the screen. "It's Kerris," I said to Flynn, but he wasn't buying it. His back leg thumped on my shoulder with a sense of urgency he'd never displayed before.

"What is it? What are you seeing?" It was a shot of Kerris talking with Carmella Highwater. They were standing on the footpath along the shore, the rotunda in the distance. Flynn urged me to bring the camera closer, so close he could touch it. Holding it up to him, he used his paws to zoom in on the rotunda, squeaking the whole time.

"Oh, someone is in the rotunda?" I asked, and he nodded, then pushed the camera away. I looked at the zoomed in screen. The image was distorted and blurry, but I could just make it out.

"It's Fay," I whispered. The long blonde hair, the black jeans, the high heels. Unmistakable, despite being out of focus. And the person she was talking to… Dino Cittadino.

"What's Fay?" Doris's head poked out from beneath the towel. "You want me to call her?" Doris was reaching for her phone when I snaked my hand out and pinned hers to the table.

"No."

"Ow!" Doris tugged her hand out from beneath mine and rubbed it. "What was that for?"

"Do not call Fay." I turned the camera so she could see the screen.

"Oh look, it's Fay." Doris smiled, then the smile slipped and her eyes narrowed. "And Dino."

"Yet she said she didn't know him."

"I wonder what they were talking about?"

"Picture's too degraded to see their expressions, but body language says…" I trailed off, my mind suddenly blank. I should know how to read body language, but right now all I had was an empty void where that information should be.

"Gimme that." Doris took the camera from me. "Fay is defensive. Her arms are crossed over her chest. She's slightly turned away. She's uncomfortable. As for Dino, his stance is non-threatening, which is curious. He has his hands out, palms up. I wonder if there's any more?"

She swiped to the next photo. "Bingo."

We uncovered a series of photos that, when put together, were like a flip card of Fay's interaction with Dino. Fay started out defensive and protective but soon turned aggressive, poking Dino in the chest. But even more interesting was that he let her. He made no move to block her, and he didn't retaliate. Few people could get away with poking a Tarkath mobster without retribution.

"All in all," Doris said, lowering the camera, "I'd say the two of them were having an argument. That's what the body language says, but without seeing their facial expressions, it's hard to say how intense it was."

"Fay got physical, poking him in the chest," I said. "That tells me it was pretty intense."

"Agreed."

"We need to get this to Calder."

"We're working with the cops now?"

I leaned forward. "Think about it. Fay was here with us. She had access to Dino's phone. She spilled coffee on the powder I'd swiped from Dino's body, making it unusable, therefore unidentifiable."

Doris slumped back, her face revealing her shock. "You think Fay Tality killed Dino?"

"Maybe? Doris, I'm sorry. I know she's your friend, but you said it yourself. She left Gravestone years ago and never looked back. She's grown up. Changed."

"Into a killer?" Doris cried, launching to her feet and pacing. "I just can't believe it."

"If it'll make you feel any better, we can give this information to Luke. Let the SIA handle it."

"None of this makes me feel better. Shower's free. You should get cleaned up." She plucked the poultices off my knees and peered at the wounds. "Healing nicely. Try not to take any more skin off."

Swinging my legs to the floor, I grimaced. "I'll do my best."

Using the bathroom in Doris's guest bedroom, I stood under the spray, pondering over our discovery. Did Fay kill Dino? Just because she had an argument with him and lied about knowing him didn't mean she killed him. I was slipping. What did we really know about Fay Tality? Other than what she'd told us, I'd done nothing to verify if what she'd said was true.

Ignoring the Christmas baubles dangling from the ceiling and the tinsel draped over the mirror, I stepped out of the shower and wrapped myself in a towel. I'd have to put on the same sweaty clothes, but at least the blood from my scrapes was gone, and like Doris said, they were healing nicely. The magic infused poultices worked wonders.

I was dried and dressed when I realized I'd left

my walking boot in the dining room and if anything needed a wash, that thing did. Opening the bedroom door, I hesitated when I heard voices. Had Calder dropped by to check on us? My heart did its usual little skippty-skip-skip, and I headed down the hallway with a smile on my face and anticipation in my hobbled step when I skidded to a halt.

It wasn't Calder talking with Doris. It was Fay. Pressing my back to the wall, I inched closer, ears straining to eavesdrop.

"Seems like we're going to do this the hard way," Fay was saying, then a loud crack, the sound of flesh meeting flesh with high velocity. Cautiously, I peeked my head around the corner, stunned at what I saw. Doris was tied to a chair, the red imprint of Fay's hand clearly visible on her cheek.

Clamping a hand over my mouth to stifle the gasp threatening to escape, I considered my options. Charge in and rescue Doris or retreat and call for help? The deciding factor was Flynn, sitting beneath the dining table out of sight, signaling that Fay was holding a gun. That made up my mind for me. Neither Doris nor I was bulletproof.

My eyes dropped to my walking boot that had fallen from its position propped against the table leg and was now obscured half beneath the table, half beneath the chair I'd been sitting on. A score in my favor. Fay did not know I was here. She thought Doris was alone. I nodded at Flynn and slowly retreated down the hallway to the guest bedroom, almost jumping out of my skin when Flynn streaked ahead of me.

Easing the door closed, I looked at Flynn and whispered, "She's got a gun?"

He nodded.

Pulling out my phone, I was about to dial Calder when Flynn tapped my bare foot. He shook his head, pointed to his ear, then the door.

"Right. She might hear me. We have the element of surprise. Best try to keep it that way." But I couldn't stand the thought of her hurting Doris. And for what? The Shadowfall Amulet? Or that we were closing in on revealing she was a killer? Which we didn't have proof of, not yet anyway. Which then begged the question, why was she here beating up on an old lady?

I nearly hit the roof when the phone in my hand started ringing. The ringtone blared out at one hundred decibels while I grappled to keep a hold of the vibrating beast and silence it before Fay heard. It was Calder, and I sent up a little prayer of apology for rejecting the call. I was all thumbs as I hurriedly typed out a message.

S.O.S. Doris in trouble. Can't talk.

I'd just hit send when I heard the creak of a floorboard outside the door. Fay had heard. Deciding my best course of action was to play innocent, I flung open the door and smiled at her.

"Oh hi, Fay, I didn't know you were here."

She didn't return the smile. Instead, she raised her arm, and I found myself staring down the barrel of her gun. "Cut the crap," she said. "Get moving." She jerked her head toward the dining room.

"What's going on? Why the gun?"

"Shut up!" She shoved me in the back, and I staggered forward, my foot twinging, my knees protesting. I had seconds to act, to take her down. Because if I let her tie me to a chair like she had Doris, well, then we'd both be powerless, and I couldn't have that.

"Ow!" I cried, doubling over and clutching at my leg, pretending I was hurt. Well, more hurt than I already was.

"Holly?" Doris cried from the dining room.

"What's wrong with you?" Fay shoved me again,

but I dug my heels in, refusing to move. "Get moving."

"I've got a broken foot, you stupid woman," I hissed through my teeth. "I'm not wearing my walking boot, so yeah, excuse me for being in pain."

"Where is it?" She sighed. By her tone, I imagined it was accompanied by an eye roll.

"I left it in the dining room."

"Well, you're just going to have to manage without it. It's not far."

"Have you ever walked with a broken foot?" I snapped.

"You're going to have more than a broken foot to deal with if you don't get moving," she snarled, then pressed the barrel of the gun to the back of my head.

"Really? A gun to my head. How am I even a threat to you?" I was talking to distract her and it was working. The pressure on my skull eased, and I took a chance. I pulled the S.I.N.G. maneuver. The elbow to her stomach had her letting out a satisfying "ooofffff" noise, the heel to the instep didn't achieve a whole lot since I was barefoot, the fist to the face was most satisfying—if not painful on my knuckles—and I didn't bother with the groin because Flynn took over, scampering up Fay's back to cling to her head, his little claws digging in while she screamed and danced around with a rodent stuck on her head.

She dropped the gun, and I scooped it up, training it on her while she screamed hysterically and tried to pull Flynn off. All she managed to do was rip out strands of her own hair, long blonde tresses falling to the floor. I was horrified until I realized they were extensions.

"Okay, Flynn, I've got this," I said. Flynn gave Fay a parting swipe across her forehead, leaving behind three long scratches, before he leaped to the floor.

"Ow," Fay hissed, pressing her palm to her face, feeling the stickiness of her own blood.

"Your turn to move. Into the dining room, now." I jerked the gun at her, and she eyed me up and down.

"Careful with that," she said. "It's loaded."

"Don't worry, I know how to handle a weapon."

"Holly love, lo—" Doris called, followed by a muffled sound I couldn't make out. I figured Doris was trying to get out of her restraints.

"Everything's okay, Doris." Pressing the gun into Fay's back, I forced her into the dining room, only to stop in surprise when I discovered Luke standing behind Doris, one hand resting on her shoulder.

"Oh good, you're here. That was fast. Did Calder send you?"

"Nope."

"No? Okay, never mind. You're here now. That's all that matters." I pointed to a chair and ordered Fay to sit. Luke stayed where he was, standing behind Doris. "Why aren't you moving?" I asked. "Untie Doris."

"He's with her," Doris said.

"What?"

"He's. With. Her," Doris enunciated. "They are in it *together*."

That's when Luke aimed the gun he'd had hidden behind Doris's back at me. I returned the favor, stepping back from the chair Fay was sitting in and training my gun on him.

"Drop the gun," he ordered.

"Seems we're at a stalemate," I said. "I'm not dropping my gun. I suggest you drop yours."

"Do you even know how to shoot that thing?" Luke drawled, a smirk curling his lip.

I frowned. "What? Of course I do. I'm an SIA agent, just like you."

Fay snorted out a laugh.

"Why are you laughing?" This wasn't a laughing matter, and the fact that they were laughing at me told me they knew something I didn't. Something they thought highly amusing. Something I was bound *not* to like.

"I told you they did a number on her, didn't I?" Luke said to Fay.

Tired of their games and suspecting they were trying to distract me, I strengthened my resolve and my grip on the gun. "Drop the gun," I repeated.

"Holly, or should I say, Tess?" Luke began. "There are some things you don't know."

"Yeah, I figured that much," I snapped. "Why don't you fill me in? Starting with how you two came to be working together. It was you, Fay, wasn't it, who killed Dino?"

"I removed his heart from his chest, yes," she said, voice eerily calm, and despite the heat, I shivered, for there was a coldness to her, a sense of evil that practically emanated from her pores. How had we not noticed it before?

"Why? As a sacrifice to open the Obsidian Field?"

"Because he was my father, and he had to die."

I looked at Doris, who was as shocked as I was. "Dino Cittadino was your *father*?" Doris gaped at the blonde woman with scratches on her face and arms. Of Flynn, there was no sign.

"He got my mother pregnant and abandoned us.

Mom died in childbirth. He should have stepped up. He didn't. He had to pay."

Oh my God! I mouthed at Doris. All this time, we'd thought Dino's murder was occult related, a blood sacrifice of some sort. Instead, he died at the hands of his vengeful daughter for abandoning her as a baby.

"With his *life?*" I mean, there's extreme and then there's extreme.

"Enough of this," Fay snapped, surging to her feet, keeping her back to me. I jumped back, swinging my gun from Luke to Fay.

"Do not move!" I yelled. "I *will* shoot you."

"Go ahead." She turned to face me, arms open wide. "Do you even know how to take the safety off?"

To be honest, I hadn't given it any thought, but the mechanics of a gun were second nature to me. SIA standard issue was a pyre gun, but the revolver in my hand worked along the same principles. Or so I figured.

"Why do y'all keep asking me if I know how to use a gun?" I grumbled, keeping it trained on her, suspicious of their motives. They were playing with me, toying with me, presumably hoping to distract me enough that they'd get the jump on me like I'd gotten on Fay. Although having said that, Luke could just shoot me because I'd made a colossal error and taken my focus off the man with the gun and switched it to the unarmed woman in front of me. I shifted my aim from Fay back to Luke, retreating another step, trying to keep them both within range.

"You may be SIA but you're no agent," Luke said.

"What?"

"I said, you may be SIA but you're no agent," he repeated.

I shook my head and rolled my eyes. "Yes, I *heard* you. But what do you mean, I'm not an agent?"

"Oh sugar," Fay drawled, fluttering her fake eyelashes at me. "You're the hired help."

"I'm the what?"

"You work in the kitchen."

"The kitchen?" I was confused. I glanced at Doris who was looking at me wide-eyed.

"You are a kitchen hand at SIA HQ. You work in the canteen," Luke said.

CHAPTER EIGHTEEN

"You're *lying!*" The gun wavered precariously as my entire arm shook and the enormity of what he'd said sank in. I wasn't the agent I thought I was. They'd tricked me, as part of the hex, the altering of my memories. They'd made me believe I was an SIA agent when the truth was... I was a cook.

I looked at Doris, whose eyes were full of sympathy. "You knew?" I croaked. Of course she knew. She was an agent. Retired, but still a bona fide agent.

Focus. The word echoed through my head. There'd be plenty of time to digest what they'd told me later... if it was true. So far, their capacity for telling the truth was pretty low, and I'd be a fool to allow anything either of them said distract me from the job at hand.

"Not that it hasn't been fun," Luke said, "but we need to wrap this up. Hand it over and we'll be on our way."

"Hand what over?" Movement at Doris's feet caught my attention. It was Flynn, and he was climbing up her leg. Doris twitched. Then giggled.

"What's wrong with you?" Luke glanced at her, and she quickly schooled her face before saying, "I'd take a step back if I were you, son. The prunes I had with breakfast this morning are making their presence felt. I need to fart. There might be follow through."

I had to bite my lips to keep from laughing, for Luke hurriedly backed up a step, while Fay looked at her askance.

"What?" Doris glared at her. "Don't think you don't have this in your future, missy."

"Enough of this nonsense." Fay turned back to me, ignoring Doris and totally missing Flynn, who was chewing through the ropes binding her to the chair. "I've searched your house, and it's not there, therefore it must be here. Save us all some time and tell us where it is."

I shook my head. "What on earth are you talking about?"

"Don't play dumb, Holly. Your face gives you away every single time. The Codex of the Solstice. I know you have it."

"I don't have it," I protested. Fay responded by sweeping her arm across the dining room table, sending the condiments and knickknacks that had been sitting in the center flying.

"Don't think I won't destroy this house, piece by piece, until I find it," Fay threatened.

"Go ahead." Doris snapped. "But you won't find anything. Oh, but I lost a blue dangly earring a while ago. If you find it, I'd be grateful."

Fay raised her hand to strike Doris, and I stepped forward, the gun steady in my hand, my aim true. "Do not touch her! And do not think that I won't pull the trigger, because I will, and even a novice can't miss at this range."

Luke pressed his gun into the back of Doris's head. "Neither will I."

Fay laughed, the sound jarring to my ears. Magic surged through my body, and instead of pushing it down, I let it have free rein. What did it matter, anyway? The whole hiding out in Gravestone because there was a bounty on my head and they could trace my magic thing had been a ruse, therefore I could see no reason why I shouldn't use the one thing I knew and trusted. My magic.

Keeping the gun trained on Fay's chest with one hand, I dropped the other, feeling my power build. My hair stirred from an invisible breeze, a warmth spread over me, as if I were basking in the sun. I wanted to spread my arms wide and tilt my head back, but I didn't dare, knowing Luke would probably shoot me.

"Search the kitchen," Luke said to Fay.

When it looked like she was about to obey, I snapped, "Stay right where you are."

"Don't worry about her. She's not going to shoot you," Luke drawled. "And if she does, well, I'll shoot her friend here."

I glanced at Doris, who was watching me closely. *Ready?* she mouthed. I gave a slight nod. *In three?* I nodded again, then with my hand by my side, I counted down using my fingers.

Fay decided Luke was right and headed toward the kitchen. She was directly between me and Doris when I got to three and let my magic loose. Using my left hand, I manipulated the air. Wind, coming from nowhere, whipped my hair around my head, and Fay squealed as she was caught in a mini tornado that picked her up, slammed her into the wall, and pinned her there.

Doris, arms free from her bindings, reached back and deftly disarmed Luke. Between one blink and the next, the gun went from being in his hand to hers. Jumping to her feet, she turned, the gun aimed at his head. Over the sound of the wind and Fay screaming, Doris yelled, "Don't think I won't shoot. Because I will. And I'd get a great deal of pleasure from it. So, go ahead. Make a move. Heck, just breathe too heavy and I'll put a nice round hole right between your eyes."

Luke was dumbfounded, and I took advantage, shooting a blast of magic his way, knocking him off his feet and skidding him backward across the floor until he crashed into the wall. His head slammed into the doorframe, rendering him unconscious.

Doris grinned at me. "Nice." Keeping her gun aimed at Luke, she stepped backward toward me, placing her hand over mine and gently sliding the gun out of my hold and tucking it into the back of her pants.

"He's out cold," I said.

"He could be playing possum," she said. "And I refuse to be fooled again. Once is more than enough." Keeping the gun trained on Luke, she grabbed the gnawed ropes from the floor around her chair and tossed them to me. "Tie him up, Holls."

"Pleasure."

Luke really was out cold. As soon as I reached his side, I nudged him with my foot, and he slumped even farther to the floor, where I rolled him onto his stomach and tied his hands behind his back. I examined the knots I'd used. "Will this hold?" I looked over my shoulder at Doris, unsure of myself.

Her face softened. "Holly Day, don't buy into their BS."

"Are you saying they lied and I *am* an SIA agent?" Because if that were the case, these two were excellent liars, for I'd totally bought it. Somehow it had rung true to my ears.

"Of sorts." Doris shrugged.

"What does that mean? I either am or I'm not."

"Put it this way. You *do not* work in the kitchen."

"Doris," I grumbled, straightening. My foot hurt, my knee ached, and above all else, a headache throbbed behind my left eye. "How about you just tell me the truth and we can get on with things, yeah?"

She rolled her eyes, and her head bobbled, but she said, "Fine! You're an analyst. You are an analyst for the SIA."

"An analyst? Of what?"

She shrugged. "Whatever needs analyzing, I guess? I don't know. When I was SIA, I was out in the field. The analysts were in-house. But know this: you were definitely trained. Analysts complete basic training, so yes, you know how to restrain a perp. Or shoot one."

"Ladies, if you don't mind," Fay yelled to be heard over the wind. "Could someone get me down?"

"I've got this," Doris assured me, so with a swivel of my fingers, I released Fay and called my magic back, watching as Doris grabbed Fay's arm and forced her onto a chair. Rolling my shoulders and stretching my neck, I smiled. It felt good to use my magic again, like going for a run after you've been sidelined by an injury for weeks. It felt even better that we'd beaten the bad guys.

Outside, sirens approached, followed by the screeching of tires and slamming of car doors. Calder kicked in the front door, weapon drawn as he charged inside, Deputy Biden hot on his heels.

"Really, Calder?" Doris said. "You couldn't have just turned the knob?"

His eyes swept over Luke, out cold and tied up on the floor, to Fay, tied to the chair Doris had been restrained in earlier. "Sorry, Doris. Holly's text said SOS, and I'd just received Dino's phone records."

"Oh?"

"Fay Tality and Dino Cittadino exchanged a lot of calls and text messages. She lied about knowing him. I put two and two together."

I glared at Fay. "When you cracked his phone, you deleted all traces of yourself! But if you came here to kill your father, why are you with him?" I pointed to Luke, who was stirring.

"It was a two birds with one stone type situation," Fay said, seemingly unperturbed that she'd been caught. "When Luke heard that a witch in Gravestone was trying to open the Obsidian Field, he did a little research into the Shadow Binder Covenant. He suspected the Codex of the Solstice had already been found—by you." She shot me a look, but I refused to give her the satisfaction of a reaction. I stared back at her, a herculean effort to keep my face blank. I'm not sure I pulled it off, since my face and I usually have issues communicating.

"It didn't take much to plant a suggestion with the mayor that a treasure hunt in Gravestone would be good for the town, giving Luke and me the cover we needed."

It was coming together in my head. "Wait. You've

known all along that Dino was your dad. So, you probably knew about his relationship with the mayor—business or otherwise. Is that how you got to the mayor? Through Dino?"

"Not me. Him." She jerked her head toward Luke, whose eyes were open, his wrists flexing against his bindings. They held, and I breathed a sigh of relief.

"Luke has been working with the Tarkaths for years," Fay continued. "He told Dino about the Shadow Binder Covenant, suggested that he mention hosting a treasure hunt to Kerris. Of course, she ran with it like it was her idea. It didn't take much to get Jensen Chapman to invite me, nor bring Luke onboard in his undercover capacity, representing the charity."

"Did you know she was Dino's daughter?" I asked Luke.

"Negative." He wriggled and maneuvered himself upright, leaning against the wall behind him, legs stretched out in front.

"How did you know her, then?"

He looked at me like I was an idiot. "Because she's Tarkath, and like she said, I've been working with them for years."

I stared at Fay, astonished. "You're a member of the Tarkath Syndicate?" I hadn't expected that. But then I hadn't expected that Dino was her father, and she was the one who'd ripped his heart out.

She shrugged. "Family bloodline."

"And Dino's heart? Did you need that for the spell?"

Fay laughed derisively. "No. I needed it for my collection."

Luke snorted. "You should see her collection. Row upon row upon row of jars."

"Don't tell me—all of them containing the hearts of the people she's killed," Doris said. "How decadently evil of you."

"Wait," Deputy Biden whispered to Calder. "Is she saying she's a serial killer?"

To be honest, I'd forgotten the deputy was there. Before Calder could answer, Deputy Laura Biden charged forward, handcuffs at the ready. "Fay Tality, I'm arresting you for the murder of Dino Cittadino… and possibly others."

"You have the right to remain silent because whatever you say will probably be stupid anyway," Doris added, arms crossed in satisfaction.

Luke smirked, watching the deputy haul Fay to her feet and march her outside to the waiting patrol car. "Cute little thing," he sneered. "Doesn't know about the SIA, does she?"

"Doesn't matter. Either way, the two of you are going to the cells until SIA comes to collect you," Calder said, helping Luke to his feet and steering him to his truck out front. "And don't think of staging a break-out. The cells are reinforced, SIA approved."

Doris and I followed, watching from the front lawn, Flynn on my shoulder.

"They sure opened a can of hot water," Doris said, wrapping an arm around my waist.

"What?"

"Luke and Fay. When they decided you were an easy target. You know, growing up, I never thought Fay was the sharpest egg in the attic, but it seems there's more to that girl than any of us ever realized."

"Her being a member of the Tarkath Syndicate, for one."

"We need to call this in." Spinning on her heel, she headed for the splintered front door.

"Wait." I limped after her. "Call it in to who?"

"The SIA, silly."

"But they already know... don't they?"

Doris absently waved an arm, ignored the mess in the dining room, and headed for the kitchen and the coffeepot. "No, I mean for you. We need to speak to the director. Find out what happens next."

I sank into a chair and leaned my elbows on the table, holding my head. The headache that had started up behind my eye had not progressed, but it hadn't eased either. At least I wasn't puking up my guts on Doris's dining room floor, which I took as progress.

Flynn scampered up my leg and leaped onto the table, patting my arm in what I could only call sympathy. I looked at the now yellow rat. "Did you really place a protection spell on me?" I whispered.

He nodded.

"Even though you knew that using your powers, your magic, would trigger the hex and turn you into a rat?"

He nodded again. My eyes blurred, and a tear overflowed, trickling down my cheek. Flynn stood on his hind legs and wiped it away.

"Thank you," I choked. "Is there any way we can reverse it?"

He shrugged, then shook his head.

"Oh, Flynn." My voice wobbled. "I'm so sorry."

"Hey, hey, hey." Doris placed a cup of coffee in front of me. "What's with the waterworks? We got the bad guys."

I smiled weakly and wiped the moisture from under my eyes. "I was just having a Flynn moment."

"He'll be fine. Won't you, Flynn?" Doris ran her hand over Flynn's back, and he nodded in agreement. Taking her seat, Doris placed her phone in between us on the table and dialed. "It's on speaker."

I nodded, ignoring the pit in my stomach, which was at odds with the butterflies. This was it. I was about to learn my fate. Had my time at Gravestone come to an end, now that the truth was out? Was I about to be pulled back to HQ, leaving behind my new best friend and the man who made my heart do somersaults in my chest?

"SIA. How may I direct your call?"

Heart hammering so fast you'd think I was running a marathon, my skin bathed in sweat, I reached to snatch up the phone. My one thought? Disconnect. I wasn't ready. I wasn't ready for my new life to end.

CHAPTER NINETEEN

"Nate Wilder." The deep, hypnotic voice on the other end of the line held the type of authority you'd expect from the director of the SIA. I hadn't believed Doris could reach him, that he'd even agree to speak with us. Only she had, and making sure the phone was out of my reach so I couldn't attempt to end the call—again—she said, "Hello, sir, this is Doris Shutt. Thank you for agreeing to talk with us."

"I've been briefed on the situation in Gravestone," he said. "Thank you for calling in, Doris. Is Tess with you?"

I cleared my throat. "I'm here. Although I'm Holly now. Holly Day."

Two seconds of silence passed. "Cute name. Doris, is this line secure?"

"Affirmative."

"Then it would be my pleasure to debrief you."

My heart was beating so fast I thought I was going to pass out. I couldn't breathe, couldn't draw enough air into my lungs. Doris touched my arm, and I almost hit the roof. I stared at her, eyes wide, and she mimed drawing in a deep breath. I mimicked her, taking a breath, holding it, before releasing it in a whoosh. Then another. Slowly, my vision cleared, my heart rate settled, and the panic receded just enough that I could semi-function.

"Holly, I understand your memories have been altered?"

"Yes," I croaked.

"Are you all right?" The concern in his voice was evident. I wished I remembered him, but the truth was, I didn't. I didn't remember anything about my time in SIA HQ. But he sounded like a nice man, a man who cared about his team, and I appreciated that.

"I'm fine." I rasped. "Nervous."

"In which case, I'll get on with it. So, Holly, your role in the SIA is as an agent in the relics and artifacts branch, and it was through your work that you discovered the Shadow Binder Covenant and the fact that they were potentially still active."

"Through your research, you determined the Shadowfall Amulet, one of the items needed to open the Obsidian Field, was located in Gravestone. That's when we discovered a leak in the SIA because you were attacked in a suspected kidnapping attempt. We believe those responsible wanted to force you to use your talents to find the amulet."

I looked at Flynn, who hadn't taken his eyes off the phone, listening intently to Nate.

"That's when you came up with the plan to travel to Gravestone yourself. Be *on the ground*, so to speak."

"It was *my* idea to come here?"

"Correct. While you were working the case from Gravestone, we were working it from this end while trying to find the mole here."

"What I don't understand is why you wiped my memories. How was I meant to work the case if I didn't remember there was a case to work?"

"I didn't authorize that."

I glanced at Doris, shocked.

"Who did?" she asked. "Scott Harding?"

"Scott Harding has been relieved of duty," Nate said, a hint of steel underlying his words. I got the impression the director was not impressed with how Scott Harding went about his duties. "His methods go against everything the SIA stands for."

"Wait!" I jumped in again. "Is Scott Harding a person? Or a coven?" Luke had told me Scott Harding was the name of the SIAs coven of witches. But I was learning fast that Luke was an exceptional liar and had put his own depraved twist on things.

"The SIA doesn't have a coven of witches." Nate confirmed my suspicions.

"And I don't come from an ancient line of witches that has the power to open the Obsidian Field." It wasn't a question. Luke had played me, and I'd bought it, one hundred percent.

"Is that what Agent Campbell told you?" Nate asked.

"If Agent Campbell is Luke Bizzy, then yes. He told me Scott Harding wasn't a person but a coven and that I was descended from the original witch who created the Shadowfall Amulet and the Codex of the Solstice and my blood was needed, along with those items, to open the Obsidian Field."

The sound of papers shuffling crackled through

the phone, then Nate said, "From your own research, Tess—sorry, I mean Holly—that isn't true. There is no need for a witch or blood. The items themselves are already spelled. There is no need for further magic.

"A team has been dispatched to retrieve Agent Campbell and his accomplice." Nate said, continuing on as if the cold hard truth he was laying at my feet weren't a complete bombshell.

"Fay Tality," Doris supplied when I remained silent. "Once a resident of Gravestone, but since moved away. She's a member of the Tarkaths. A very active one by the sounds of things. You should find her lair. I believe she kept trophies of her kills."

"Noted. Was there anything else?" Nate asked.

"The Shadowfall Amulet," I said. "We searched for it in the caves, but someone else beat us to it. So, it's out there, somewhere. This hasn't gone away."

"Sheriff Calder has been in touch," Nate replied. "Fay Tality had the amulet in her possession. The team will collect it from the sheriff when they pick her up, and it will be secured in the vault. There is no way the Obsidian Field can be opened. Even if the Codex of the Solstice turns up, it's of no use without the amulet."

"About the Codex," I said, clearing my throat. "I may know where that is."

Nate was silent for a moment, then said, "I'll instruct my team to make contact with you. Well done, Agent Hunter. Sheriff Calder made sure I was aware of how helpful you have been to local law enforcement."

My cheeks heated at the compliment. "What about Gavin Flynn?" I blurted, glancing at Flynn, who had barely moved a muscle since the call started. "He triggered a hex when he protected me."

"I've been made aware of Agent Flynn's heroic actions. Is he with you now?"

"He is."

"Agent Flynn, first of all, thank you. The SIA does not take your sacrifice lightly. You triggered your hex to protect another agent, and while I'm sure our thanks doesn't mean a lot to you right now, just know that by doing that, you helped out a mole in the SIA and bring down a member of the Tarkaths."

Flynn squeaked, an abrupt noise that I took to be *thanks*.

"Also, know that we are actively searching for a way to reverse the hex. Actually, Holly, we would like your assistance on that front. Your expertise and knowledge are invaluable."

"It would be my honor, sir."

"Which brings me to my next point. John Smith provided an excellent cover story for you, but the truth remains that the gates to Purgatory remain unguarded."

I glanced at Doris, who winked at me, then turned her attention back to the phone. She'd remained suspiciously quiet throughout the call, which was very uncharacteristic of Doris.

"Sir, with all due respect," Doris finally spoke up. "How is that an SIA issue?"

"If it affects the supernatural world, it's an SIA issue. From what I understand, Holly, your memories are somewhat…" He paused, searching for the right word.

"Sketchy," I supplied.

"Right." I could practically hear him nodding. "Which, unfortunately, means you are not fit for duty."

I wasn't sure whether to be relieved or outraged. "Are you saying I can't come back to work until my memories are restored?" What if that never happened? There were no guarantees my poor Swiss cheese brain would ever fully recover. Had I just been fired?

"I'm saying we'd like you to remain in

Gravestone in the capacity of temporary gatekeeper until we can find someone to fill the position permanently. The SIA is working with the Council on this issue, but until we can get it resolved, we need a gatekeeper."

"She'll do it," Doris said, while I sat like a goldfish out of water, my mouth opening and closing, but no words coming out. Eventually, I squeaked, "Doris!"

Nate chuckled. "You know how this works, Doris. I need to hear it from Holly. Of course, she'd need to maintain her cover. And that of whatever resources she thinks she'd need to assist Agent Flynn with his hex problem."

Doris nodded and flung her arms around me, indicating the phone and encouraging me to do something useful. Like speak.

"I'll do it," I finally croaked, then looked at Doris, tears in my eyes. Ever since arriving in Gravestone, I'd been counting the days until I could leave, but then I'd met Doris. And Calder. And those two people had very quickly become the most important people on earth to me. And despite not remembering much about my life, I somehow sensed I'd never had this before. Friendship. A sense of community.

And then there was Flynn, who'd torn his

attention away from the phone to look at me. I gave him a wobbly smile and held out my fist. He dutifully stretched up and gave me the cutest fist bump.

"Agents, was there anything else?" Nate asked.

"The mole. Was it Luke? Or Harding?" Doris asked.

"Agent Dwayne Campbell—aka Luke Bizzy—was the mole. Agent Scott Harding was unfortunately a victim of Campbell's manipulation."

"Before you go—I cleared my throat—"my broken foot. Harding told me it couldn't be healed and given half the things I've been told turned out not to be true, I was wondering…"

"Of course. I'll have a medic sent to you. Anything else?"

"Ask him about a pay rise," Doris hissed, and Nate chuckled, overhearing her.

"Since you are technically stepping into a role outside your original employment contract, you will, of course, be re-numerated appropriately."

"House renovations?" Doris asked.

"Fully renovated and furnished on the SIA's tab," Nate said. "I believe, while John Smith had a vehicle at his disposal, it's not exactly roadworthy?"

"Oh my God, you're getting a car," Doris

squealed, then quickly slapped a hand over her mouth. "Sorry," she added in a whisper.

"A vehicle would be useful, sir."

"Then we're agreed. Expect a team within the hour. Ladies, thank you for your service, but now I really do need to run. I'm late for a meeting."

"Thank you, sir," Doris said, and then we were listening to the dial tone. Doris turned to me. "You get a car!"

I nodded, my face stretching into a wide smile. I was getting used to smiling. When I'd first arrived in Gravestone, it had felt so foreign, stretching my face muscles in such a way. But since meeting Doris, I'd been doing it more and more frequently. "I get a car," I agreed. Then it hit me. Not only was I getting a car, but Nate Wilder, the director of the SIA, had just authorized John Smith's house to be fully renovated and furnished on the SIA's tab. Of course, he didn't know that I'd already started. I'd gone with the theory it was better to apologize than to seek permission.

Doris jumped to her feet and grabbed my hands, pulling me out of my chair. Standing in her dining room, holding hands and grinning like loons, we said in unison, "I'm staying!" "You're staying!"

THE END

While you wait for the next installment of the Gravestone mysteries, check out **Ghost Mortem**, book one in the Ghost Detective series: www. janehinchey.com/ghost-mortem

AFTERWORD

Thank you for reading, if you enjoyed **What the Hex**, please consider leaving a review. You can find a complete list of my books, including series and reading order on my website at:

www.JaneHinchey.com

Also, if you'd like to sign up to receive emails with the latest news, exclusive offers, and more, you can do that here:

www.JaneHinchey.com/subscribe

And finally, I'd love to invite you to join my **VIP Readers group** where you get exclusive access to me, the opportunity to win one of the monthly signed paperback giveaways, join in live videos, get sneak peeks at works in progress and so much more.

www.JaneHinchey.com/LittleDevils

Thank you so much for taking a chance and reading my book - I do this for you.

xoxo

Jane

The guest list for the shifter party Kristina Gates is catering has just turned into a suspect list—for murder.

When Ted McNeil is found dead at a high society event, it looks at first like he choked on one of Kristina's cupcakes. But it soon becomes evident that foul play was involved. The cupcake was poisoned.

Kristina's determination to salvage her reputation and learn the truth launches her quest to appease the Witches' Council and avoid a life sentence in the pokey. With the help of her fae friends and sexy Watcher Ben Hoffman, she untangles a web of lies that threaten her very existence.

Faced with a mysterious foe, a family of tight-lipped shifters, and a competitor who would stop at nothing to put her out of business, Kristina realizes nothing is as it seems and the shadows hold secrets that some would kill to keep.

Get a copy of Cupcakes & Curses for FREE as a thank you for joining my newsletter! Sign up here: www.JaneHinchey.com/subscribe

ABOUT JANE

Jane Hinchey is an Aussie author who loves to write cozy mysteries with plenty of laughs and mayhem along the way - who says murder can't be fun? Her bestselling Ghost Detective series combines all of this into an intriguing melting pot of paranormal danger, fast-paced action, and plenty of tongue-in-cheek snarky humor.

Jane lives in the mortal realm with her non-paranormal man, two cats whose paranormal status is yet to be determined (she did catch them trying to open a portal in the kitchen that one time), a turtle named Squirt (who is massive!).

Sometimes, when the supernatural chaos calls for a different kind of story, she writes under the name Zahra Stone, where the characters you meet are as sexy as they are deadly.

Learn more or sign up for her newsletter at
www.JaneHinchey.com

facebook.com/janehincheyauthor

#1 One Minute to Midnight

#2 Two Minutes Past Midnight

#3 Third Strike of Midnight

PARANORMAL ROMANCE/URBAN FANTASY

The Awakening Series

#1 First Blade

#2 First Witch

#3 First Blood

Ingram Content Group UK Ltd.
Milton Keynes UK
UKHW041513240323
419044UK00017B/97

9 781922 745231